The Cat's Meow

by Steven Peros

A SAMUEL FRENCH ACTING EDITION

SAMUEL FRENCH

FOUNDED 1830

NEW YORK HOLLYWOOD LONDON TORONTO

SAMUELFRENCH.COM

ISBN 978-0-573-69624-4   Printed in U.S.A.   #29028

IMPORTANT BILLING AND CREDIT REQUIREMENTS

THE CAT'S MEOW was first presented by Rialto Entertainment at The Coast Playhouse, in Los Angeles, California, on October 19, 1997. It was directed by Jenny Sullivan; the setting was by Bill Eigenbrodt; the lighting by J. Kent Inasy; the costumes by Christine Tschirgi; and the hair & make-up by Judi Lewin. The Line Producer was John Peros and the Stage Manager was Kevin Carroll. The cast was as follows:

WILLIAM RANDOLPH HEARST . . . . Albert Stratton

THOMAS INCE . . . . John C. Mooney

MARION DAVIES . . . . Kim Bieber

ELINOR GLYN . . . . .Pamela Gordon

CHARLIE CHAPLIN . . . . Joseph Fuqua

LOUELLA PARSONS . . . . Nancy Cartwright

At some performances by Von Rae Wood

MARGARET LIVINGSTON . . . . Marianne Ferrari

GEORGE THOMAS . . . . Tim Van Pelt

JOSEPH WILLICOMBE . . . . .Steve Tyler

DR. DANIEL GOODMAN . . . . David Bickford

MRS. GOODMAN . . . . Von Rae Wood

At some performances by Nancy Kandal

CELIA MOORE . . . . .Tracie May

DIDI DAWSON . . . . Precious Chong

MRS. INCE . . . . Von Rae Wood

At some performances by Nancy Kandal

CHARACTERS

(in order of appearance)

ELINOR GLYN - 60, British romance novelist, screenwriter, and social dictator.

THOMAS INCE - 40s, a silent film pioneer and studio mogul.

MARGARET LIVINGSTON - 20s, an actress and mistress to Ince.

GEORGE THOMAS - Ince's business manager.

MARION DAVIES - 27 (but passing for 23), a movie star and Hearst's public mistress.

CHARLIE CHAPLIN - 35, British, an internationally known movie star.

(**NOTE:** Ince and Chaplin should be roughly similar in height and build)

LOUELLA PARSONS - 40s, a Hearst movie reviewer from the East Coast.

WILLIAM RANDOLPH HEARST - 62, Newspaper and silver mining magnate. A large, wealthy, powerful, married man.

JOSEPH WILLICOMBE - Hearst's loyal and discreet personal secretary.

DR. DANIEL GOODMAN - 40s, former physician, now a Hearst movie studio executive.

MRS. GOODMAN - 30s, Dr. Goodman's conservative wife.

CELIA MOORE - 20s, a flapper/actress.

DIDI DAWSON - 20s, also a flapper actress.

MRS. INCE (VOICE ON PHONE) - 40s, Ince's recently awoken wife, who remained at home.

(**NOTE:** For "Mrs. Ince", some productions have had an actress appear on stage, with a phone in her hand. If this method is utilized, doubling is possible with "Mrs. Goodman")

TIME AND PLACE

The action of the play takes place in November of 1924 on board William Randolph Hearst's yacht, The Oneida.

The play should be performed with one intermission.

THE SET

The play can be effectively performed with a two-level set, but it is not required for a successful production.

If two levels are possible, even by the use of rear risers, then the stage level would be used for the arrival deck scene (I:1), after which the dining table and chairs should be brought on and remain for the entirety of the play (NOTE: Stage hands should be dressed as ship's stewards, and behave as such, to maintain fluidity). The elevated level would have two cabins, at right and left, and a Captain's Wheel center, allowing Hearst to steer, looking out over the audience. If a permanent Captain's Wheel is possible, then Hearst may appear at the wheel at the opening of the play, steering, until his entrance. A steward may take the wheel when unattended by Hearst. The cabins can be fully designed or merely suggested by a single small bed. The cabins would be used for I:4, II:1, II:6

If a single level set is used, the dining table should be set for I:2, struck for I:4, and reset at intermission where it will remain until final curtain. The suggestion of a cabin, even just a bed, should be brought on for Scenes I:4, II:1, II:6.

Regarding the dining table, this need not be thought of literally as one long table. It can be modular, or two tables at a ninety-degree angle, with the angle pointed upstage, or two separate tables allowing room for characters to rise and walk about. If space is an issue, the table need not seat all thirteen cast members and thjere may be fewer chairs. Despite what is indicated in the text, some characters may be on their feet, drinking, mingling, flirting, standing behind a seated guest.

Plates and tableware need not be used as the dining room scenes are pre-dinner and after dinner, though champagne glasses are required for I:3 and II:3. Scene II:7, indicated as breakfast, need only have a few coffee cups and a bowl of fruit, set by Stewards.

ACT ONE

Scene 1

*(A light finds **ELINOR GLYN**. Her English voice is smooth, refined.)*

ELINOR. Black. And White. Black is the absence of color. In white, there is the entire spectrum. Hold a clear prism up to white light and you get a rainbow. Hold that same prism up to black and you get...Oh hell, more black. I am a writer. My art has one tool. Words. Black ink on white paper. People often speak of Truth being black and white. Still others say that we dream in black and white. Art. Truth. Dreams. Darkness coupled with so many colors. Come with me will you? Tell me if what I dreamed is true. Or if my truth...is but a dream. Come. We are about to go yachting...on the grayest ocean you've ever seen.

(SCENE: THE DECK OF THE ONEIDA)

(At stage left is the top of a gangplank from which each of the arriving guests enters.)

*(**THOMAS INCE** enters. He is a short man with a large handsome face and a head of wavy hair. After a beat, **MARGARET LIVINGSTON** enters, an attractive actress. On her arm is **GEORGE THOMAS**, Ince's middle-aged business manager.)*

MARGARET. My God, look at the size of this thing. It must be two hundred feet long.

INCE. Two-twenty.

MARGARET. He *owns* this thing?

INCE. And the ocean it's sitting in. And the sky.

GEORGE. Some of his more minor holdings include City Hall, Washington, and the Police Force.

INCE. Oh yeah. Those little things.

GEORGE. Maybe the old boy will give you the ship as a present, Tom. We could sell it and use the cash to start getting your studio out of hock.

INCE. No one's in hock. Not yet anyway.

GEORGE. Just wait 'til those year-end projections catch up with us.

MARGARET. Well you can't do a damn thing about it on a cruise to San Diego.

INCE. Margaret's right, George. Look on the bright side. Mr. William Randolph Hearst has invited us all on his yacht for the express purpose of celebrating *my* birthday.

GEORGE. That and a quarter will buy you a ticket to the movies.

INCE. He controls more newspapers and magazines than any man in the country. Chock full of exciting contemporary stories. He also has quite a lot of other assets in motion pictures that could be of use to us.

GEORGE. Yeah – cash. *(then, seriously:)* Are you planning to make a play for Hearst this weekend?

INCE. Me? I wouldn't be so pushy. Let's just say it's a birthday gift the old man doesn't know he's giving me yet.

(MARION enters, spotting INCE's figure from behind.)

MARION. Charlie!

(INCE turns around and MARION realizes her mistake.)

MARION. Dopey me – Tom! *(She gives him a hug.)* Happy birthday to you, happy birthday to you –

INCE. My birthday's not 'til tomorrow, but I love it when a pretty girl sings to me. Where's our Captain?

MARION. Oh you know Willie. He's up there in the Captain's station like it's Mount Olympus, watching the mortals arrive. 'Be right back with His Greatness. *(And with that, she exits.)*

(CHAPLIN steps onto the deck.)

INCE. Charlie, how are you?

CHAPLIN. Busy, very busy.

INCE. Same here, same here. You know George Thomas, my business manager. And this is Miss Margaret Livingston, George's guest and a delightful actress in her own right.

CHAPLIN. *(to* **MARGARET***)* Charmed. *(back to* **INCE***)* And *Mrs.* Ince?

INCE. Couldn't make it – one of our boys isn't feeling well.

CHAPLIN. *(looking* **MARGARET** *over skeptically)* Hmmm. I am sorry to hear that.

GEORGE. *(deflecting attention from* **MARGARET***)* Say, that "Woman of Paris" was a terrific picture. Pretty big risk you took by not appearing in it.

INCE. Yes sir, you're a risk taker, Charlie, just like me. Just when you got everybody laughing with your Little Tramp character, you go and make some weepy melodrama without him! Well, you can't fault a man for taking a gamble. Failure is a character-builder, eh Charlie?

CHAPLIN. Yes, a character builder. If you'll excuse me.

*(***CHAPLIN** *beats a hasty retreat to the buffet table.* **MARGARET** *watches him go.)*

MARGARET. Thanks a lot. You introduce me and then you hog him to yourself.

INCE. *(re: Chaplin)* Little prick.

GEORGE. Really? I hear he's got a pretty big one.

INCE. An actor running a studio. It's like the goddamned serfs running the palace. He lost his shirt on that last picture and they say he's so overbudget on "The Gold Rush" that his financiers aren't returning his phone calls.

GEORGE. Not to mention that his *sixteen year-old* lead actress collapsed on the set – pregnant.

INCE. Really? They learn about the birds and the bees so much younger these days.

GEORGE. The buzz around town is that Chaplin did the pollinating.

*(And with that, **GEORGE** follows **INCE** and **MARGARET** OFF as they stroll the deck.)*

*(**MARION** returns, balloons in hand, with which she proceeds to decorate. She ignores **CHAPLIN** who pops one of her balloons in order to get her attention.)*

MARION. Why haven't you returned any of my telephone calls, you little shit.

CHAPLIN. Because I hate telephones and I knew I'd see you this weekend.

MARION. Maybe I was calling to tell you to stay away this weekend.

CHAPLIN. That would pretty much ensure my arrival, wouldn't it?

MARION. Willie's heard about us. He's even had private detectives poking around. He invited you this weekend so he could watch us. In fact, he's up there watching us right now. Nothing can happen this weekend, do you understand me? Nothing.

CHAPLIN. So what are you doing next weekend?

MARION. Jesus Charlie, how much more direct can I be? You didn't get me into bed and you're not going to. It's gotta stop. *Now.*

CHAPLIN. Says you or says Mr. Hearst?

MARION. Says me.

CHAPLIN. Has the old man turned you completely off romance?

MARION. Come off it, Charlie. If you married every girl you wined and dined, you'd have six hundred wives.

CHAPLIN. More or less. But that's ended now.

(He steps toward her intimately. She pulls back stiffly.)

CHAPLIN. To Hell with Willie and his suspicions. Isn't it punishment enough that I have to banter with his dullest assortment of guests yet? Tom Ince and his birthday entourage – you know he's having an affair with that Margaret person.

MARION. I thought she was with that George someone or other, his business manager?

CHAPLIN. Darling, I've indulged long enough in similar situations to recognize who is cheating on whom and with whom the cheating is being done.

MARION. Especially since you're usually one of the "whoms."

(**LOUELLA** ["**LOLLY**"] **PARSONS**, *arrives, decked out in her best attempt at "California chic" clothing. Nervous, she stands at the gangplank with a bedazzled expression fixed painfully on her face.*)

(**INCE**, **MARGARET** *and* **GEORGE** *return from their stroll.*)

MARION. I better go help our little Miss Lollipop before people start hanging their coats on her.

(**CHAPLIN** *stops her before she goes.*)

CHAPLIN. Marion. Do you really believe that if you had reached me, I would have stayed away?

MARION. No. But you should really believe that I wanted you to. *(crosses to* **LOLLY** *and then turns to her guests)* I won't have anybody walk on this boat without being introduced to everybody. Lolly, this is Everybody. Everybody, this is Lolly – Miss Louella Parsons, the insightful movie reviewer for Willie's "New York American." Especially insightful because of the wonderful things she writes about me!

LOLLY. And I wrote them even before I knew that you and Mr. Hearst were…I mean, that you two are…that you're both…uhm…

(You can hear a pin drop as all eyes are fixed on **LOLLY**. *She is aware that she's inserted her foot in her mouth. Finally:)*

LOLLY. Gosh this thing is big, isn't it?

(From behind her, a deep, eloquent woman's voice booms forth.)

ELINOR. Yes dear, but does he know how to use it?

(All heads turn to see the arriving **ELINOR**. *The guests laugh at her remark. Tableaux.* **ELINOR** *addresses the audience.)*

ELINOR. Welcome to Hollywood – a land just off the coast of the planet Earth. I have traveled the world and lived almost everywhere, yet I remain in this place. I fear this bizarre yet fascinating town, but I can't leave it. You see, I'm never quite certain if I am visiting the zoo or if I am one of the animals in a cage. *(a beat)* This yacht belongs to William Randolph Hearst. That woman is Marion Davies, his very public mistress. It is November, 1924. Thirteen passengers *walked* on board; one of us was *carried* off horizontally two days later. Little evidence exists to support *any* version of the weekend events. History has been written in whispers. This is the whisper I hear in my dreams.

(End Tableaux. Action resumes.)

MARION. Louella Parsons of The East, meet Elinor Glyn of The West. Elinor is the finest and naughtiest author in the entire world.

LOLLY. You don't have to tell me that. I wish I could be introduced as being "Of The West."

ELINOR. Whatever makes you happy, dear.

(She hurries to **CHAPLIN**. **LOLLY** *follows closely behind.)*

ELINOR. Hello, you little bastard.

CHAPLIN. It's the "little" I object to.

(They kiss with genuine respect and affection. **LOLLY** *breaks in.)*

LOLLY. Mr. Chaplin, it is an honor, and I mean a true honor to meet you, sir. Did you happen to notice the rave review I gave your last picture, "A Woman of Paris"?

CHAPLIN. Yes, I did. Thank you. It was very kind.

LOLLY. So deserved, so deserved. It just stinks that no one went to see it. Well, I'm sure you won't lose your shirt on the next one, too. *At least* you have the sense to be *in* this new picture. *(musing over the title)* "The Gold

Rush" – I hear that title's just a hint as to how much the picture's costing you.

ELINOR. Well, I'll leave you two then. I have a…oh something-or-other to attend to.

(**ELINOR** *slips away, leaving* **CHAPLIN** *trapped in* **LOL-LY**'s *literal clutches*)

CHAPLIN. I really should be –

LOLLY. You know, Charlie, this is my first visit out west. Writing Motion Picture Critiques is one thing, but if I'm truly going to make a difference, what I need is a daily column, with my name on top, marking the place where both the people in the audience *and* the people on the screen can look to read The Truth, not just vicious rumor and gossip.

CHAPLIN. Well, keep after old W.R. – I'm sure he'll come around.

LOLLY. Oh I plan to, believe you me. I mean, take you for example. I want you to know that I, for one, am soooo sorry about the…"personal problems" you're going through with this costar of yours, this…little girl, Lita. If you ever want to confide in someone sympathetic to your needs – I'm all ears. After all, you'll need someone on your side when the shocking news breaks.

CHAPLIN. Why thank you ever so much, Miss Parsons.

LOLLY. Lolly.

CHAPLIN. Pardon?

LOLLY. "Lolly" – all my *close* friends call me Lolly.

CHAPLIN. *(with barely concealed revulsion:)* Lolly…

ELINOR. Charles! Come over here this instant or I will pummel you to the ground!

(**CHAPLIN** *breaks away from* **LOLLY** *and crosses to* **ELINOR** *just as* **WILLIAM RANDOLPH HEARST** *makes a grand entrance followed by* **JOSEPH WILLICOMBE**, *his personal secretary, clipboard in hand.*)

HEARST. Welcome!

(**ELINOR** *and* **CHAPLIN** *editorialize confidentially.*)

ELINOR. Such a remarkable economy with words for a man who controls more print than Jesus Christ.

CHAPLIN. *(with mock outrage)* Elinor! I will not tolerate such comments at Mr. Hearst's expense. Take it back or I will dishonor your good name.

ELINOR. I do hope *someone* dishonors my name – I'm feeling rather frisky.

(Just then, DR. and MRS. DANIEL CARSON GOODMAN, an older conservative couple, step onto the deck.)

DR. GOODMAN. Permission to come aboard? *(He laughs loudly as he helps his wife board.)*

CHAPLIN. Who?

ELINOR. Dr. Daniel Carson Goodman. Only Hearst would conceive the profane notion of appointing a physician as a movie studio executive. Old W.R. invites them to remind himself that for every one of "us" there's *two* of "them."

CHAPLIN. What is the wife's name?

ELINOR. Who knows.

MRS. GOODMAN. My word! What a big boat!

ELINOR. Correction: who cares.

(back to INCE and GEORGE)

GEORGE. Hearst is a tricky fish, Tom. He's known to nibble and back off.

INCE. That's the difference between you and me, George: you'd stop at hooks and worms. I'd use a goddamned harpoon with poison on the tip if I could get my hands on one.

(WILLICOMBE approaches HEARST.)

WILLICOMBE. Chief, it's just past noon. We should keep on schedule, if we can.

HEARST. Raise the gangplank!

(Just then, two young flappers, CELIA MOORE, and DIDI DAWSON, dash onto the deck just as the gangplank is being taken away.)

CELIA. He always does this to us, every time! Just to see us run!

DIDI. I'm sweating like a pig. How am I gonna land anyone with sweat dripping off my nose?

CELIA. Don't bitch, Didi, I'm not in the mood.

(Out of HEARST*'s view,* CHAPLIN *takes* MARION*'s hand and kisses it. She snatches her hand away. Only* INCE *witnesses this.* GEORGE *leers at the two flappers.)*

GEORGE. I think this is going to be a most enjoyable boat ride.

INCE. *(his mind on what he has just witnessed)* Yes...the cat's meow.

HEARST. That's it everybody! Out to sea!

(The lights fade as the Oneida sets sail.)

Scene 2

(The main Dining Room on board The Oneida. A long exquisite table with thirteen chairs. Bottles of ketchup and mustard are incongruously strewn throughout the fine china and silver. The room is empty as the lights come up.)

*(After a few moments, **ELINOR** enters.)*

ELINOR. Good God! I will not be seen arriving on time.

(She does an about-face and exits.)

*(**LOLLY** enters. She sets her gaze on an empty seat and begins to speak, as if someone were sitting there.)*

LOLLY. Mr. Hearst, writing motion picture critiques for you is an honor. However, I feel there is a pot of gold lying at the end of the proverbial rainbow that – sonofabitch! *(She shakes her head sharply and takes a deep breath, before starting again.)* Chief, we are both consummate professionals, immensely skilled at what we do. Like your desire to branch out into politics and movies, so too do I feel a need to expand my – shit, shit, shit!

*(From offstage, the sound of a single gunshot. **LOLLY** freezes, listening. Two more gunshots sound in succession. **LOLLY** makes a frightened exit.)*

*(**HEARST** enters the room holding a diamond-studded revolver and a gun box. He proceeds to clean the gun throughout much of the following. **INCE** enters, concerned.)*

INCE. Did you hear gunfire?

HEARST. Seagulls.

INCE. Pardon me?

HEARST. Seagulls. It's the best time of day to get a few. Three for three.

INCE. Oh…I see.

HEARST. You gotta keep the gun low, or else they see it.

INCE. Right, right, of course. *(a beat)* Is there somewhere you'd like me to sit?

HEARST. I love movies, Tom. Years ago, we thought that the greatest power a communicator could possess was the press. It's just not true anymore. The press relies on the limited language of words; and words don't always translate well across seven continents – believe me, I know. No, Tom, the moving picture is the new – and maybe ultimate – "Great Communicator." Sure there are a few subtitles to read, but through those pictures…those glorious moving pictures…a universal language filled with morality, politics, and any other goddamned thing I want to stick in someone's head is at my fingertips. I'd love to be around in a hundred years and see what we've done with them.

(A moment or two passes.)

INCE. Can I be…frank with you, W.R.?

HEARST. You can be whoever you like, Tom.

INCE. I think you are the greatest newspaper man this country has ever seen. I also think your eye for movies is right on target. But you must face facts: there are some things you cannot control.

HEARST. Like what?

INCE. Your political and family life – even your newspaper empire – is based on the East Coast. The movies are here on the West Coast, where I am.

HEARST. I'm aware of that.

INCE. Then you should also be aware of your limitations as a movie producer. You can't send orders over the telephone and you can't have yes-men represent you when real decisions have to be made.

HEARST. You are being almost…inexcusably frank.

INCE. Only because I think you have a major talent in Marion Davies and a brilliant head for the motion picture world. All you need is a "hands-on" guiding force to oversee spending, production, –

HEARST. And that's you?

INCE. W.R., I've made millions from this business and we both know that despite the enormous quality of your pictures, you've never made back a dime. There is a lot of money in movies, W.R.

HEARST. Yes. Mine. (*a beat*) All right, suppose I agree with all your "frank observations." Are you implying that Thomas H. Ince can make things different?

INCE. I'm not implying it, W.R., I'm stating it. And I'm not just talking about Cosmopolitan Pictures renting my studio space, I'm talking about personally overseeing Cosmo – and Marion in particular.

HEARST. How personal?

INCE. Consulting with you on which scripts and directors are right for her, making sure she has the finest co-stars, keeping her productions cost effective –

HEARST. What's in it for you?

INCE. The stories in Cosmopolitan and your other magazines, for starters.

(**HEARST** *pauses to absorb all that has been said.*)

HEARST. Tom, it's not that I doubt your background in the movie business. On the contrary: that's just where it is lately – in the background. Even you have to admit that you're not the force you were five, ten years ago.

INCE. That may be true – of both of us, perhaps – but we each have different strengths to help the other's weaknesses.

HEARST. No offense, Tom, but when and *if* I'm in trouble, I don't need a cripple to help me up.

(*Just then,* **WILLICOMBE** *and* **DR. GOODMAN** *enter.*)

HEARST. Dan! Joe! I don't think you've met my guest of honor. Tom Ince, this is Joe Willicombe, my personal secretary and Dan Goodman, one of my executives over at the studio.

(*The* **THREE MEN** *exchange greetings and handshakes.*)

You and Dan should get acquainted. Joe, can I have a word with you?

*(As **HEARST** steals away to a stage left corner with **WILLI-COMBE**, the other guests begin to filter in. First **ELINOR**, **DIDI**, and **CELIA**.)*

DIDI. Only one drink per person? What kind of party is this?

CELIA. *Presidents* answer to him for God's sake! Are you telling me he can't get us some good bathtub hooch?

ELINOR. Well, dear, it is technically illegal.

DIDI. Yeah, but not for *us*.

*(**GEORGE** and **MARGARET** enter the room along with **MRS. GOODMAN** and **LOLLY**. **INCE** excuses himself from **DR. GOODMAN** and pulls **GEORGE** away from **MARGARET**, leaving her standing alone. The two men talk inaudibly.)*

*(Back to **HEARST** and **WILLICOMBE**, who have been speaking.)*

WILLICOMBE. No, she's not in her room, Mr. Hearst.

HEARST. Well whose room *is* she in?

WILLICOMBE. I'll try to find out.

HEARST. Do it fast. I don't know what the hell to do with all these people.

*(back to **GEORGE** and **INCE**)*

GEORGE. "I don't need a cripple." He actually said that to you?

INCE. Nice way to treat the guest of honor, huh? If I had the same mean streak, I'd throw that fling Marion and Chaplin are having right in his face.

GEORGE. Marion and Chaplin?

INCE. I saw them holding hands on deck. Have you noticed that they're the only people we're waiting for at the moment?

*(The **TWO MEN** look over at **HEARST** who appears to be counting heads)*

INCE. Look at him? He's figuring out who's here and who's not. In a moment he'll come to the same conclusion I have.

GEORGE. Well, I advise you to just keep it to yourself.

INCE. I know, I know. I'm a decent man, George.

*(**MARION** enters, just seconds ahead of **CHAPLIN**.)*

*(The proximity of their arrivals does not go unnoticed by **HEARST**…or **INCE**, who elbows **GEORGE**.)*

MARION. *(addressing the room)* Don't tell me you were all waiting for little old me to get the festivities started?

ELINOR. Marion, dear, since you and Charles have decided to grace us with your presence, would you have the decency to tell us where to sit?

MARION. *(standing at the stage right head of the table)* Oh this is the fun part. If Willie had it his way, he'd talk business all night. Isn't that right, Tom?

INCE. Whatever you say, Marion.

MARION. You, Mr. Birthday Boy, will sit way down at *my* end of the table and talk absolute nonsense all night. Willie, you stay put –

*(**HEARST** takes his seat at the stage left head of the table.)*

– and why don't we have Charlie sit by you to keep you laughing all night.

CHAPLIN. Or is that vice versa?

*(**CHAPLIN** moves towards an empty seat nearest **HEARST**.)*

MARION. Now, Charlie, hold your tongue.

*(As **CHAPLIN** sits, **HEARST** pulls his chair out from under him, causing him to land on the floor.)*

HEARST. *And* your seat.

*(**HEARST** lets out a roar of laughter. **CHAPLIN** looks at him, not quite sure what to make of the prank. He slowly rises, **HEARST** and the other guests still laughing.)*

*(**CHAPLIN** chooses to join in, flashing a smile at **HEARST**.)*

CHAPLIN. Got me fair and square, W.R. I've done it to many in my films, but never had it done to me in real life.

HEARST. How does it feel?

CHAPLIN. *(realizing he's being challenged and not willing to give an inch)* Envigorating.

(The guests all move to their seats, engaging in indiscernible conversation.)

(Lights Fade.)

Scene 3

(The main Dining Room – same as the previous scene – an hour later.)

(The seating arrangement is as follows: **MARION** *is at the head of the table at stage right. Continuing towards stage left is* **INCE, DIDI, WILLICOMBE, ELINOR, MARGARET, CELIA, MRS. GOODMAN, GEORGE, DR. GOODMAN. LOLLY, CHAPLIN,** *and* **HEARST** *at the stage left head.)*

DIDI. *(to* **WILLICOMBE***:)* So, who are you exactly?

WILLICOMBE. Joe Willicombe. Mr. Hearst's Chief Secretary.

DIDI. So you're the one they call "Big Joe." *(a flirt)* Wonder why…I'm Didi Dawson.

WILLICOMBE. I know who you are, Miss Dawson. I saw "Lady of The Harem."

DIDI. You did, eh? Now what did your Mama think about *that?*

WILLICOMBE. Mama was sitting on my lap.

   *(***DIDI*** screams with laughter as our attention shifts to* **ELINOR** *and* **MARGARET***.)*

ELINOR. It's none of my business, darling, but I'd forget him if I were you.

MARGARET. Pardon me?

ELINOR. *(nodding toward* **INCE***:)* Married moguls and mistresses do not mix, Margaret. *(a beat)* Oh that's good. I must use it in a novel. Do you have a pen, dear?

   *(***MARGARET*** can respond only in stunned silence.)*

INCE. So, Marion. Not even one teeny weeny bit of business talk?

MARION. Go ahead.

INCE. I'm trying to negotiate a deal with, W.R. Tell me the secret – How do you get through to W.R.?

MARION. You wanna know my secret? *(leaning in closer:)* I don't have to do a goddamn thing.

INCE. I don't follow.

MARION. People have funny ideas about me and Pops – the whole gold-digger thing –

INCE. No, no, no – I wasn't suggesting –

MARION. The truth is it was Willie who did the pursuing. Used to buy two seats every night when I was in the Follies – one for him, one for his hat. I never once asked him to put me in a picture. Hell – it would take more effort to get him to *stop* putting me in pictures. I guess that's my secret, Tom – with Willie, I don't have to "dig."

(now, to **CELIA** *and* **MRS. GOODMAN***)*

CELIA. Your husband is Dan Goodman?

MRS. GOODMAN. Oh yes, he certainly is.

*(***MRS. GOODMAN*** throws a kiss in her husband's direction. He waves back in response.)*

CELIA. So who's that?

MRS. GOODMAN. *That's* Dr. Goodman!

CELIA. *(disappointed:)* Oh. I thought perhaps your lover was on board. Too bad.

*(***MRS. GOODMAN*** is speechless.* ***GEORGE*** turns to his neighbor,* ***DR. GOODMAN***.)*

GEORGE. Now, Dan, don't be so modest.

DR. GOODMAN. Oh no, Mr. Hearst takes full responsibility for Cosmopolitan Pictures.

GEORGE. Everyone knows you're one of his top executives.

DR. GOODMAN. That's kind of you, but you know, I'm actually a physician by trade.

GEORGE. You're a…*doctor*?

DR. GOODMAN. Semi retired.

GEORGE. Oh my. Isn't that…

DR. GOODMAN. Medicinal?

GEORGE. Not the word I was looking for, but it'll due for now.

*(***HEARST*** is speaking to* ***CHAPLIN***.* ***LOLLY*** is next to the comedian, thus close enough to eavesdrop.)*

HEARST. You know, Charlie, I've been away for a while, out of touch. I feel like I've lost sight of my motion picture properties…Marion. What do you think of how I've been handling Marion?

CHAPLIN. What do I think?

(**CHAPLIN** *looks at* **LOLLY**, *who looks away quickly, pretending not to be listening.*)

HEARST. Yes.

CHAPLIN. Can I be frank with you, W.R.?

HEARST. You can be whoever you like, Charlie.

CHAPLIN. Well, I think Marion is a wonderful comedienne. Her smile, her eyes – (*just then* **MARION**'*s laugh can be heard*) – her laugh. They all work a delightful magic when the material is right. What she *doesn't* need are extravagant sets, and gowns of silk and feathers. It does nothing but interfere with the charm of her lovely face.

HEARST. Are you saying I spend too much money on Marion's pictures? I already know that. What if I tell you it doesn't matter to me. I spent sums on her last picture that I could never possibly recoup and I suppose I'll do the same on her next one.

CHAPLIN. But it's easy to lose sight of her beauty in the clutter of your "dramatic extravaganzas."

HEARST. I don't want people laughing at Marion. She belongs in pictures that have a big world, an important world. She'd be wasting her time monkeying around with some baggy-pants clown. No offense, Charlie.

CHAPLIN. You're not doing what's best for Marion. No offense, W.R.

(*A stunned* **LOLLY** *waits with ill-concealed eager anticipation. Before* **HEARST** *can respond,* **MARION** *leaps up.*)

MARION. I propose a toast!

DIDI. (*aside, to* **WILLICOMBE**) It better be a damn good one since this is the only glass of hooch we're gonna get.

MARION. We all owe a lot to Tom. Not only did he invent the cowboy picture, but he helped build this town.

(Cheers of "Here, here" can be heard.)

MARION. He figured out how to run a studio that could make ten movies at the same time. How to direct 'em, how to produce 'em –

HEARST. Wait a minute, this is starting to sound like that picture where Buster Keaton poked a little fun at old Tom.

(The guests spark with recognition, beginning to chuckle. All but **INCE**.*)*

HEARST. Remember? "A Buster Keaton Presentation of a Buster Keaton Production. Produced by Buster Keaton, Directed by Buster Keaton…"

*(***HEARST*** *trails off, joining the guests who are all laughing. At* **INCE***'s expense.)*

MARION. Hush, Willie. To Tom!

(The guests laugh and toast. Inaudible conversations resume.)

HEARST. Look, Charlie, I know you're under a lot of pressure right now with all the problems you're having –

CHAPLIN. I can assure you, I'm perfectly –

HEARST. Say no more, my friend: apology accepted. *(turning quickly to* **LOLLY***)* So, Lolly, how are you enjoying sunny California?

LOLLY. *(seeing her opening:)* It is just so wonderful, Mr. Hearst. The more I see the lovely people who populate it, the more I'm reminded of the need for a columnist –

HEARST. You know, Lolly, the first rule of California living, as Marion keeps reminding me, is not to mix business with pleasure. I don't do it and I don't like my guests to do it. Now, you were saying?

LOLLY. I was saying that you have truly invited a boat full of the most interesting people I've ever met in any one place.

HEARST. See, Charlie? That's why I hired her: even with a gun at her head she still gives me unconditionally rave reviews. (**LOLLY** *smiles as* **HEARST** *laughs heartily.*) Well, guns at our head aren't so bad. Keeps the blood flowing.

CHAPLIN. As long as no one pulls the trigger.

(**HEARST** *thinks a beat and then bursts into a thunder roar of laughter. Several of the guests notice.*)

MARION. What are you laughing about down there?

LOLLY. It was the funniest thing ever! All about a gun at my head and the trigger going off!

(**LOLLY** *screams with laughter. The rest of the guests stare at her with polite smiles, but no laughter.*)

ELINOR. Well, I suppose you had to be there.

MRS. GOODMAN. Guns and triggers – such violence!

CELIA. All in line with Madame Elinor's California Curse.

LOLLY. California Curse? What's that?

MARION. Oh not that nasty thing. Not now.

CHAPLIN. Yes, Elinor, do educate the visitor in our midst.

ELINOR. Well, Lolly dear, The California Curse strikes you like a disease the moment you arrive in Hollywood, so pay close attention.

LOLLY. *(enraptured)* I am, I am.

ELINOR. You see, Lolly, this place you've arrived in, this place we call home, is not a place at all…but a living creature.

MRS. GOODMAN. A living creature?

ELINOR. More precisely – an evil wizard. Like in the old stories.

LOLLY. And you all…live on him?

CELIA. Like fleas on the belly of a mutt.

ELINOR. Exactly. Except unlike a helpless dog, this Evil Wizard is able to banish the true personalities of those whom he bewitches, forcing them against their will to carry out his command, to forget the land of their birth, the purpose of their journey, and whatever principles which they may have once held dear.

DIDI. Don't forget about the symptoms of the disease – that's my favorite part!

ELINOR. You know the curse is taking hold if you experience the following symptoms: you see yourself as the most important person in any room; you accept money as the strongest force in nature; and, finally, your hold on morality…vanishes without a trace.

*(**ELINOR**'s recitation stops the table conversation dead in its tracks. **HEARST** is extremely uncomfortable.)*

CHAPLIN. Well, thank goodness none of *us* have been infected, eh, W.R.?

*(**HEARST** doesn't know how to respond. Sensing the tension, **MARION** jumps up.)*

MARION. Charleston, Everybody!

*(From offstage, the ever-ready band strikes up a rousing Charleston. The guests welcome the digression and leap to their feet to dance. **MARION** grabs **HEARST**.)*

MARION. Come on, Pops, let's show 'em how it's done.

(She pulls him to the dance floor. He makes a valiant effort, but his size prevents him from looking graceful.)

*(**DIDI** charms **WILLICOMBE** into a dance. **MARGARET** turns obligingly to **GEORGE**. **LOLLY** dances alone… embarrassingly.)*

*(**HEARST** stops dancing, out of breath but smiling, putting his arm out to **MARION**.)*

HEARST. I'm tired. Let's sit.

MARION. Sit? I want to pound my feet so hard the Devil will complain!

*(**MARION** breaks away in a joyous twirl, grabbing **DR. GOODMAN** and Charlestoning with boundless energy.)*

*(**CHAPLIN** sees his opening and cuts in, filled with equal youthful vigor and trademark grace.)*

(**HEARST** *watches, his gaze getting stonier and stonier as, conversely, his guests become more and more carefree.* **INCE** *stands at the sidelines, noticing all that is going on between* **HEARST**, **MARION**, *and* **CHAPLIN**.)

(*The lights slowly fade to darkness.*)

Scene 4

(Two beds are set up symmetrically, one at stage right representing Marion's State Room, the other at stage left representing Margaret's State Room.)

*(Center is **HEARST** at the wheel of the ship, staring out over the audience as he steers. The lights will rise and fade on **HEARST** as indicated throughout, but he should always be in some sort of partial illumination.)*

*(As the lights come up, **MARION**, **ELINOR**, **CHAPLIN**, and **DIDI** are entering Marion's State Room. Unbeknownst to them, **INCE** is upstage center, witnessing the entourage enter the room.)*

*(The lights are down on **MARGARET**'s State Room.)*

MARION. *(withdrawing a bottle of liquor from under the bed)* Who's first?

DIDI. *(snatching the bottle)* If anyone touches that before I do, I'll give 'em a fat lip.

ELINOR. *(as **DIDI** swigs mercilessly)* Who says femininity is dead?

DIDI. *(lowering the bottle)* Marion, you still have the best moonshine in all of California.

CHAPLIN. At Marion's bungalow, every day is Valentine's Day – bottles filled with lust arrive on the hour from her many admirers.

DIDI. Well this one's sure got sex appeal. Who gave it to you?

CHAPLIN. *(providing the pay-off for his premeditated set-up)* Who do you think?

*(**CELIA** enters the room holding what appears to be a small jewelry box.)*

CELIA. Marion, honey, you didn't tell me I had to provide for these deadbeats.

DIDI. Who are you calling a deadbeat? What have you got there, Celia?

CELIA. It's dope, Didi, okay?

MARION. Will you keep quiet.

DIDI. You had that with you the whole car ride and didn't tell me?

CELIA. Look, honey, W.R.'s parties can be counted on for incredible food, hot music, and great guests, but the old tea-totaller doesn't exactly offer the latest in after-hour delights, no offense Marion.

MARION. *(taking* **CELIA***'s box)* Believe me, I know it all too well. *(noticing* **ELINOR***'s disapproving scowl)* Now, Ellie, you aren't going to be a flat tire about our playtime, are you?

ELINOR. Marion, dear, do as you like. Just don't expect me to join you in such infantile nonsense. *(With that,* **ELINOR** *takes a healthy swig of moonshine.)*

(Lights fade on Marion's State Room and rise on **HEARST** *alone at the wheel, staring dead ahead.* **INCE** *enters the scene behind him. As they talk,* **INCE** *remains right over* **HEARST***'s shoulder, watching the older man's every response as he keeps his eyes fixed beyond the audience, out to sea.)*

INCE. Hello there.

HEARST. Tom, how are you?

INCE. Stuffed! That was some banquet.

HEARST. Wait until tomorrow – Marion's prepared quite a birthday feast.

INCE. Marion is a special woman.

HEARST. Yes, she is.

INCE. You're very lucky to have her.

HEARST. I know that.

INCE. *(a pause)* It's so frightening to love someone in our business, in this town. There are so many men who pray on beauty. Not sincerely, but in cruel ways, just for the conquest. Take a character like Chaplin – a creative genius, but absolutely notorious when it comes to women. I'm sure you've heard about this girl, Lita, his lead actress who collapsed on the set of "The Gold Rush" – she's pregnant with his child and she's sixteen years old, for God's sake. *(a beat)* That's why I keep my wife Nel as far away from show people as possible. I know it's ironic, since I myself qualify as "show people," but what's a man to do? She was an actress when we married, but as soon as William was born fifteen years ago, I pulled her right out of that world and securely into our home. Women simply aren't as strong as we are. They're easily fooled. Their hearts are easily reached...easily corrupted.

HEARST. Yes...it is a...concern.

INCE. It must be, especially given the amount of time you're forced to spend nearly three thousand miles away from her. *(a beat)* This might be something else I can help you with.

HEARST. What do you mean?

INCE. Well, if we merged out motion picture interests, along with all the benefits we discussed earlier...I could keep an eye on her for you.

HEARST. *(turning to face him for the first time in the conversation)* What makes you think she needs to be watched?

(**THE GOODMANS** *suddenly enter the scene.*)

DR. GOODMAN. Is four a crowd?

HEARST. Not at all. Please join us. You were saying, Tom?

INCE. We'll talk later, W.R. Goodnight, everyone.

(**INCE** *exits.*)

MRS. GOODMAN. What a nice man.

HEARST. Yes...very nice.

MRS. GOODMAN. It's a shame his wife couldn't be here.

DR. GOODMAN. I've met her once or twice. A lovely woman.

HEARST. Wives...*(His attention returns to his guests.)* I admire your marriage, Dan. So simple...clean.

DR. GOODMAN. Thank you, W.R.

HEARST. Nothing...complicating things.

DR. GOODMAN. Quite frankly, I feel particularly uninteresting next to the..."colorful lifestyles" of your other guests. Lord knows what they're all up to at this hour.

MRS. GOODMAN. Daniel, I won't hear of such talk. After all, the codes of decent behavior are still something to be held in high regard. We should feel no shame for not being as "liberal-minded" as the rest of the company.

DR. GOODMAN. Darling, please –

MRS. GOODMAN. I mean no disrespect, Mr. Hearst, but do you know what one of these actress persons said to me at dinner tonight?

HEARST. What?

MRS. GOODMAN. She had the gumption to ask if Daniel was my lover!

DR. GOODMAN. No.

MRS. GOODMAN. Yes!

DR. GOODMAN. What did you tell her?

MRS. GOODMAN. I said, "Dr. Goodman is my *husband*, deary – we are *not* lovers."

DR. GOODMAN. Well you set her straight.

MRS. GOODMAN. The thought of such a thing!

(Lights fade to partial illumination on HEARST *and* THE GOODMANS.*)*

(The lights come up on MARGARET*'s State Room. Dressed only in a slip,* MARGARET *and* INCE *are kissing passionately while they stand. As* INCE *kisses her neck, she moans with pleasure.)*

INCE. *(gently)* Shhhh…

MARGARET. *(a beat)* Did you just "shush" me?

INCE. Well, I…we're right by the door and…you were a little loud –

MARGARET. *(breaking away)* Jesus Christ, Tom!

INCE. *(not gently)* Shh. Does everyone have to hear you?

MARGARET. Yes!

INCE. Margaret, will you be sensible please.

MARGARET. I thought this time was going to be different. I thought you said I was going to come off of George's "pretend arm" and on to yours.

INCE. You will, you will. We've just got to find the right moment. We've got to be delicate.

MARGARET. No one cares whether or not you're having an affair. Look at Hearst and Marion, for Christ's sake!

INCE. *Mrs.* Hearst knows all about Marion, doesn't approve of divorce, but *has* approved the "arrangement." She wants to stay a very rich woman with the last name of Hearst.

MARGARET. Oh, so now it's your innocent, vulnerable wife Nel who's the excuse.

INCE. *(speaking quietly so that she will too)* I'm in the middle of a deal with Hearst and it's important that I not get on his morally objectionable side.

MARGARET. *(loudly)* The man's whole life is morally objectionable!

INCE. You're loud. *(loudly:)* You are loud.

(MARGARET calms down, sitting on the bed.)

MARGARET. You get me crazy sometimes. I'm sorry.

INCE. *(sitting next to her, his arm around her)* No, I'm sorry. You're right. I'm not giving you a chance to strut your stuff with these people –

MARGARET. I don't want to strut my stuff for these people. I just want to strut *with you.*

INCE. See, there you go, selling yourself short. You're a fabulous actress and you should be given a chance to shine. We can't be pushy is all I'm saying. Let me work some of my magic on Hearst and then we'll get you noticed.

MARGARET. As an actress or on your arm?

INCE. The lady places a tall order, but just maybe we'll manage both. Okay?

MARGARET. *(with a trusting smile)* Okay.

INCE. That's my girl.

(They kiss. They kiss again, more heatedly as the lights fade.)

(As the lights rise on Marion's State Room, **ELINOR** *is facing us, taking an enormous toke of a marijuana cigarette. As she releases the smoke she declares:)*

ELINOR. Time for charades!

CELIA. *(a French accent:)* Oo-La-La – Charades!

(The rest of the occupants of the room are also partying, thus, their behavior is affected by consumption of both alcohol and dope. **CELIA** *is performing a moody and sensual dance solo.)*

*(***ELINOR*** picks up three pieces of paper.)*

ELINOR. I prepared these earlier. We'll have Marion and Charles on one team. Celia and Didi will be Team Number two.

CELIA. What a gyp.

DIDI. I'll have you know I'm of championship caliber.

*(***ELINOR*** places the three slips of paper in Celia's now-empty jewelry box and holds it out to* **MARION**.*)*

ELINOR. Come, Marion. Choose!

(A very stoned **MARION** *and* **CHAPLIN** *rise before the equally "high" group. She selects a piece of paper and then pulls* **CHAPLIN** *to extreme downstage right, out of earshot.)*

MARION. *(reading:)* "Man discovers his reflection."

*(***MARION*** looks up at him.* **CHAPLIN** *shrugs, but nods. They return to the trio, standing opposite each other.* **MARION** *must match* **CHAPLIN** *'s every gesture since she is his "reflection." Throughout what follows, the exotic music on the Victrolla continues to play.)*

*(***CHAPLIN*** stares at* **MARION** *for a moment or two, his hand on his chin;* **MARION** *matches his position.)*

DIDI. Two medical students I once knew!

CELIA. Let them get started, will you?

DIDI. Just guessing.

*(***CHAPLIN*** puts his hand out;* **MARION** *does too. The palms of their hands touch.* **CHAPLIN** *snaps his hand*

back quickly, intrigued. He does it again, leaving his palm pressed against **MARION** *'s.)*

CELIA. "Indian Love Call," by Harbach and Hammerstein!

DIDI. Guppies!

*(***CHAPLIN*** steps forward, as does* **MARION**. *Then closer, until they are toe to toe.* **CHAPLIN** *tries to touch different areas of* **MARION** *'s body but her hand constantly intercepts his own since she is his "reflection.")*

CELIA. Concubines!

DIDI. Porcupines!

(The music continues to accentuate the sensual nature of their "charade." **CHAPLIN** *brings both of their hands together and arcs them over their heads.)*

CELIA. King and Queen Tutt!

DIDI. *(laughing)* There was no Mrs. Tutt.

(He then slowly moves his face closer to hers. Their lips are only a half-inch from touching. Their chests are touching. They are now playing a game far beyond charades.)

*(***CHAPLIN*** kisses* **MARION** *'s left eye, then her right, slowly, sensuously. Her hand drops from its position over their heads to his waist.)*

DIDI. I know! I know! *Sex!*

*(***ELINOR*** rises and separates* **MARION** *and* **CHAPLIN**.*)*

ELINOR. The charade has been…misread. Marion, dear, let us step over here so I may better explain it to you.

*(***ELINOR*** pulls* **MARION** *to the extreme downstage right corner of the stage as the lights dim slightly in her State Room.)*

ELINOR. Marion, what is happening? I know you're high, dear, but W.R. is only a deck away.

MARION. I know, I know. I promised this wouldn't happen…I promised myself it was over…

ELINOR. You need to "promise yourself" in order to resist him?

MARION. I don't know…can't think straight.

ELINOR. Good God – have you slept with him?

MARION. No…

ELINOR. *Have you?*

MARION. *No.*

ELINOR. Thank goodness. You're not in love with him, are you?

MARION. He thinks he's in love with me.

ELINOR. Charles in love. Always an amusing topic. Except for the women he destroys, that is.

MARION. I know, but he says his flirting days are over. He says he wants only me.

ELINOR. Marion, dear, I adore him, really I do. But Charles is only capable of having a monogamous relationship with Charles. He and his art are the only lovers he can remain faithful to.

MARION. I want to know I can believe him, Ellie. I want to trust all his…words before I…

ELINOR. Before you what? Marion, listen to what you're saying.

MARION. I don't know. Maybe there isn't room for anyone else. Not like Willie. He's the first man who ever had any faith in me. I know Willie's got a lot of…stuff to compete with. Sometimes I feel lost in it all. But at least he really wants me. I'm all he's got keeping him a human being. I'm like the sandbag on this big balloon. *(smiling at her own imagery)* Without me, he'd float up and up above us all until he…disappeared. *(a beat)* I think Willie would die if I left. If I'm not certain that a man would die without me, then I don't want him.

ELINOR. Do you really think Charles would die without you?

MARION. Charlie might cry his eyes out and recite a poem at my grave – one that he wrote himself…but give him a day or two and he'd be back in the market.

ELINOR. A day or two? Darling, Charles would copulate with a pall bearer if he found one even remotely attractive.

(*MARION smiles.* **ELINOR** *smiles back.* **MARION**'s *smile turns to tears.* **ELINOR** *steps in and gives her a gentle, maternal hug.*)

ELINOR. There, there…you'll find your way through the darkness…we all do eventually.

(*Lights fade on* **MARION** *and* **ELINOR.**)

(*Lights come up on* **MARGARET**'s *State Room and* **HEARST** *alone at the wheel.* **INCE** *and* **MARGARET** *are under the covers.* **INCE** *rolls over, frustrated.*)

MARGARET. What is it, baby?

INCE. I'm sorry.

MARGARET. No, don't be sorry.

INCE. It's just…

MARGARET. Talk to me. "It's just" what?

INCE. Everything. I'm seeing it all slipping away. Everything. Me. Tonight, Hearst told me I was a cripple in the picture business.

MARGARET. That's a lousy thing to say.

INCE. And that goddamn Buster Keaton thing.

MARGARET. He was just joking. But Marion said a lot of very nice –

INCE. I come from The Theatre. Producers get lots of credit in the theatre. They guide every aspect. Why should I be laughed at just because I take the same care in the picture business? Are we all supposed to lie down and let the actors run everything?

(**MARGARET** *guides him into a reclining position.*)

MARGARET. Of course not.

INCE. Is that how people see me? I was a force in this town not too long ago.

MARGARET. You *are* a force.

INCE. I need him. I need Hearst so badly. I can't leave this boat without him and Marion under my belt.

MARGARET. You'll get him. You are a great force.

INCE. You think so?

MARGARET. I know so.

> *(Aroused, he leans forward and kisses her passionately. The heat continues to escalate throughout the following.)*

INCE. Do you really?

MARGARET. Oh yes...I know it...you're a...force...

INCE. I am...

MARGARET. You are...

> *(The light dim slightly on their lovemaking as we shift attention to **HEARST** at the wheel.)*

> *(**WILLICOMBE** arrives with a message from the wire.)*

WILLICOMBE. A wire came through from the New York office. It's an item that's going to be published in tomorrow's New York Daily News.

HEARST. A Sunday column?

WILLICOMBE. Yes. Grace Kingsley.

HEARST. Christ, which one of my movies is she bashing now?

WILLICOMBE. *(a hesitation)* I can leave it here for you, if you like.

HEARST. No, no, read it to me.

WILLICOMBE. *(He'd rather not, but **HEARST**'s request has been made.)* "Charlie Chaplin continues to pay ardent attention to Marion Davies. He spent the evening at Montmartre dining and dancing with the fair Marion the other night. There was a lovely young dancer entertaining that evening. And Charlie applauded but with his back turned. He never took his eyes off Marion's blonde beauty. Miss Davies looked very fetching indeed."

> *(**WILLICOMBE** finishes. **HEARST** offers no response. There are a few painful moments of silence as **HEARST** stares dead ahead.)*

HEARST. Photos?

WILLICOMBE. Studio close-ups of each of them.

HEARST. Placed next to each other?

WILLICOMBE. Yes.

HEARST. Caption?

WILLICOMBE. "They're still seen about with each other."

(**HEARST** *is once again silent. Still keeping his gaze dead ahead:*)

WILLICOMBE. I'll just leave it for you here then.

HEARST. Fine, fine. You can go now.

WILLICOMBE. Would you like me to –

HEARST. *Get out!*

(**WILLICOMBE** *exits, leaving* **HEARST** *alone.* **INCE** *and* **MARGARET** *continue to make love under the covers.*)

MARGARET. I know it...I know it...Oh God, how I know it!

INCE. I....am...a...Force!

(Lights slowly fade to black.)

End of Act One

ACT TWO

Scene 1

(Curtain rises on **CHAPLIN** *in his cabin sitting cross-legged on a bed. He is staring at a shoe, which sits on the bed before him. He does not move. Several moments pass.)*

*(***MARION*** enters.)*

MARION. *(holding a piece of paper in her hand)* I have news.

CHAPLIN. *(his eyes on the shoe)* If you were starving and had no food at all, would you eat your shoe?

MARION. What?

CHAPLIN. Your shoe – would you eat your shoe?

MARION. *(after a moment)* Of course I would.

CHAPLIN. You would?

MARION. I'd have to pretend it was something else though.

CHAPLIN. *(a smile forming)* Something else…

MARION. And I'd *have to* boil it first.

CHAPLIN. Yes…boil it…that's very funny.

MARION. Well here's something that isn't. You and me are in the funny papers, courtesy of Grace Kingsley, New York Daily News.

*(***MARION*** hands **CHAPLIN** the piece of paper.)*

CHAPLIN. How embarrassing for Grandpa Willie – he spends all this money on private detectives and the Daily News gets the scoop – not even a Hearst newspaper.

MARION. Charlie – that came over the wire here on the boat. I found it in Willie's pocket.

*(***CHAPLIN*** is silent. Weighing the meaning of this:)*

CHAPLIN. When was it dated?

40

MARION. It's in today's newspaper but the wire came in yesterday.

CHAPLIN. Which means he knew about it last night and during breakfast today. *(a beat)* He's made no mention of it to you?

MARION. Not yet.

CHAPLIN. It's obvious he left it for you to find. What is he going to do – punch me in the nose?

MARION. Charlie, whatever it was we started has to end. If Willie asks me anything, I'm going to tell him it's all cheap gossip. I want you to do the same.

CHAPLIN. Let me make something perfectly clear, you may have to lie for *your* sake. But if that old money bag of yours ever asks *me*, "What designs do you have on my Maid Marion?" I will look him squarely in those beady eyes of his and tell him I would like to take out my erect penis – something I'm certain he is unable to do –

(She interrupts him with a tremendous slap on the face.)

MARION. Don't!

CHAPLIN. Don't what?

MARION. Don't punish me for...

CHAPLIN. Don't punish you for what? Falling in love with me? Say it. I can – I love you.

MARION. You don't love me.

CHAPLIN. Oh really? Are you convinced that you can only be loved by some broken down old –

MARION. *I don't love you!*

CHAPLIN. You don't mean that. You only hope you do. That if you say it loud enough, you'll actually believe it.

MARION. I love Willie.

CHAPLIN. No you don't – you love that he loves you. You love that he is such a constant – so unwavering in his feelings. But I can be that too – please believe that. You can have my love. I swear it. All of it.

MARION. I don't believe you.

CHAPLIN. Why not?!

MARION. *(exploding)* Did you promise *Lita* all your love too?! Did you snatch it away from *Lita* now that she's pregnant?!

CHAPLIN. My fascination with Lita is from some part of me whose sole function is to seek out ways to ruin my life.

MARION. Trying to steal me away from William Randolph Hearst isn't exactly turning over a new leaf.

CHAPLIN. It is. It's an act of bravery. My relationship with Lita…in the beginning as now…is an act of cowardice.

MARION. And the baby, Charlie?

CHAPLIN. That was a mistake. My mistake. But I can't marry her. I'll destroy her and my work. That cannot happen. I'm already in trouble with money – I won't let her put the nail in my coffin.

MARION. Charlie –

CHAPLIN. Don't forget, Marion. I'm not like you and the rest here. I was not "to the manor born." I know what it's like to be without. I know what nothing tastes like. *(a beat)* I've tried to reason with Lita, but her "tribe" won't hear of any alternate course of action.

MARION. What alternate course, Charlie? Abortion?

CHAPLIN. *(Yes, but he has no comment.)* I offered to set her up financially, to help her find a husband more suitable to her…*(a bit embarrassed)* age.

MARION. You know something Charlie – I think you're only upset with the kid because she let herself be corrupted by a heal like you.

CHAPLIN. And what have you let *yourself* become?

MARION. What do you mean by that crack?

CHAPLIN. Touched a nerve, have I?

MARION. Everything I am – *any*thing I am – I've *chosen* to be.

CHAPLIN. Don't let Willie hear that.

MARION. Willie knows who's running this show. I don't pretend for anybody. Not for him, not for you –

CHAPLIN. And not for yourself?

MARION. I'll tell you something about Willie. He's real. He's true. I give to him because *I want to* – he doesn't place a single demand on me.

CHAPLIN. Not placing a demand on you isn't a sign of love! He doesn't place demands on you because no one places demands *on possessions.*

MARION. How dare you –

CHAPLIN. Here's my yacht, here's my mansion, here's my Marion Davies, all stuffed and mounted –

MARION. Shut up!

CHAPLIN. A butterfly in a glass case. Lovely to look at, but one catch – she's dead! I'll pin her up in my awful movies, I'll pin her up in my "other" life, but Marion will never live, because if she did, she might have the sense to leave!

MARION. Charlie…why are you…

CHAPLIN. Because I love you. You wouldn't be just another planet in my universe – you'd be the sun. You wouldn't be worshipped like some statue I bought but as a passionate, vital woman who I couldn't live without.

MARION. Words…just words…

CHAPLIN. No – not words! You want something real? *(He takes her by both arms, holds her close.)* This is real – Passion is real! And I don't mean passion for yo-yo's or yachts or gin or dope or money or the goddamn Charleston! I'm talking about…I'm talking about…

*(Finally, **CHAPLIN** has run out of words. He is lost in **MARION**'s vulnerable eyes – having gotten through to her at last.)*

(They start to kiss wildly, falling back onto his bed…)

(Lights fade.)

Scene 2

*(The main Dining Room on The Oneida – same as I:3.
The room is empty as the scene begins. **HEARST** enters
with **INCE**.)*

INCE. That is an amazing engine room, W.R.. You know,
boating is my secret love.

HEARST. *(distracted)* Hm? Oh, yes...secret love.

INCE. It's so quiet. Even when you're right in there, up
close – it practically purrs.

HEARST. This boat has always made me very happy...calm.
I go into the engine room and that sound...calms me.

*(**HEARST** walks ahead of **INCE**, making minor adjust-
ments at the dinner table. **INCE** watches him, deciding
upon his next move.)*

INCE. You are a civilized man, W.R.

HEARST. That surprises you?

INCE. Quite frankly – yes.

HEARST. Why?

INCE. Because you have the power to behave uncivilized,
yet you choose to exercise control. You could use your
position to overstep the rules which most of us play by,
yet you don't. Before I would call you a "rich man" or
a "powerful man" I'd simply call you a "decent man."

HEARST. Thank you, Tom.

INCE. I'm not just saying it – I mean it completely amazed
me how civilized you behaved last night.

HEARST. When was that?

INCE. Well, let's face it, W.R., it's clear that Chaplin has
designs on Marion – not that she returns his affections
– but the nerve of him dancing so suggestively with
her last night when everyone knows what he's up to.
Well, it's...it's just infuriating.

HEARST. Yes...I have everything under control. *(a beat)*
What do you mean by "everyone"?

INCE. Everyone what?

HEARST. You said "everyone knows" – who's everyone?

INCE. Well, everyone on this boat for example. *(a beat)* My God...someone coming between two people in love. I've often thought of what I'd do if I ever found out that my Nel was having an affair. I'd fall to pieces.

HEARST. *(distant)* You always have to stay in control. *(a beat)* Yes...control. Without it...you're just like everybody else.

(Guests start to drift into the room, lost in conversation. **HEARST** *notices.)*

HEARST. Excuse me, Tom.

INCE. Of course.

(Upon **HEARST***'s departure,* **INCE** *sidles up to the arriving* **GEORGE** *and engages in silent patter as* **MARGARET** *enters, flanked by* **CELIA** *and* **DIDI***.)*

DIDI. You know, Margaret, there's a certain...unspoken bond among single women who are trapped on a yacht together.

CELIA. What Didi wants to know is: is it true you're Tom Ince's lover?

MARGARET. I beg your pardon?

CELIA. I think Tom Ince is very attractive.

DIDI. Not to mention influential.

CELIA. He's a little short, but then every man in this town is much smaller than you'd like him to be.

*(***CELIA** *and* **DIDI** *share a nasty laugh.)*

MARGARET. *(a bit dazed)* Excuse me.

*(***MARGARET** *drifts to a private corner, her mind distant, racing.* **LOLLY** *enters with two ping-pong paddles and makes a beeline right for* **MARGARET***.)*

LOLLY. Ping Pong.

MARGARET. What did you say?

LOLLY. Ping Pong.

MARGARET. Oh.

LOLLY. After dinner.

MARGARET. Ping Pong.

LOLLY. I just learned last night, but no one wants to play with me.

MARGARET. I suppose...

LOLLY. It's really rather dull.

MARGARET. What is?

LOLLY. Ping Pong.

MARGARET. I thought you wanted to play?

LOLLY. I do. I need to get better. After all, anyone who's anyone plays Ping Pong.

MARGARET. It is rather dull. I only like it because I can beat Tom.

LOLLY. Tom Ince?

MARGARET. That's right.

LOLLY. Why should it matter if you can beat Tom Ince?

MARGARET. *(after a moment)* Because Tom Ince is my lover.

LOLLY. *(stunned)* That is fascinating. I mean really fascinating. Here I am and there you are. We only just met and yet there is something about me that you instinctively trust. That's happened to me all my life. People are willing to come to me with their darkest secrets and confide in me. I keep trying to tell Mr. Hearst that people trust me. They'll turn to my page on a daily basis to find the truth, understanding. Very much like you did just now.

MARGARET. I hate to burst your bubble, Lolly, but at this moment, I would've told whoever or whatever was standing there.

LOLLY. Yes, but how lucky that I just learned how to play Ping Pong last night or else you might have told the wrong person. There are "wrong people" you know.

MARGARET. Yes, I know.

LOLLY. Don't worry, your secret is safe with me.

(LOLLY pats MARGARET on the shoulder conspiratorially and continues through the room. THE GOODMANS enter.)

INCE. I think it's going very well.

GEORGE. I hope so, for all our sakes. What sort of specifics have you discussed?

INCE. Marion.

GEORGE. Marion? The merger is the issue. The stories in his publications, his film holdings –

INCE. There is only one issue where Hearst is concerned – Marion Davies. All the rest is just a game to him.

GEORGE. Then I advise you to handle it with extreme caution. A wife is one thing, but using a man's mistress for business leverage is something that can explode in your face.

INCE. Trust me, George – if there's one thing I know, it's how to handle mistresses.

(**DR. GOODMAN** *abruptly leaves his wife's side and approaches* **WILLICOMBE**. *Given their proximity,* **MRS. GOODMAN** *addresses the equally stranded* **MARGARET**.)

MRS. GOODMAN. Hello. I'm Mrs. Goodman – Daniel Goodman's wife. I don't think we've been properly introduced.

MARGARET. Margaret Livingston.

MRS. GOODMAN. Charmed. And what is it you do, Miss Livingston?

MARGARET. I'm Tom Ince's lover.

(*Tableaux.*)

ELINOR. (*to audience*) Hello again. Soon after my ears were able to understand the chatter of adults, I was told three things. First, to respect the nobility to which I was born and look down on those who struggle to survive. Second, that there is no religion more sacred than my Christianity. And third, I was told that my red hair is ugly, unfashionable, and will prevent me from finding true love. (*a beat*) Well! (*a beat*) As for my nobility, I embraced the working man, rejected the class system, and later had it reject me when my now-deceased husband drained the family fortune dry. As for Christianity, I'm afraid a rather insipid catechism teacher failed to properly introduce me to The Father, The Son, or The Holy Ghost. There is only one belief I have come to embrace during my years on this earth, only one force in the universe that continues to prove itself to me with aggressive conviction: What goes around comes around. Them. Me. You.

(**ELINOR** *makes a move to exit, but then has a last thought.*)

ELINOR. *(cont.)* Oh yes, my red hair and its relation to true love. *(a beat)* Let's just say…I've found evidence of true love in poems, written of it my novels, smelled it like a bouquet that has been snatched from a room moments before I arrive. In short, I've heard it happens for some people. Even for those with red hair. Yes. I've heard it happens.

Scene 3

(Same main Dining Room set as above except that now, all thirteen chairs are filled with the entire cast, who all sport party hats. **INCE** *in a cowboy hat,* **CHAPLIN** *in his tramp bowler,* **HEARST** *in a self-effacing jester's hat.)*

*(***HEARST*** *is dead center,* **MARION** *and* **INCE** *are at either end.* **DR. GOODMAN** *sits to one side of* **INCE***.)*

*(***CHAPLIN*** *sits beside* **ELINOR***.* **MARGARET** *next to* **MRS. GOODMAN***. The rest in the remaining seats or standing.)*

*(***HEARST*** *is proposing a toast.)*

HEARST. A birthday toast to my good friend Thomas H. Ince. Tom is here this weekend so that we can celebrate the birthday of a giant of the motion picture world.

CHAPLIN. *(aside to* **ELINOR***)* Spare me.

ELINOR. I don't think he'll spare any of us, darling.

HEARST. And, second, so that he and I could get to know each other on a more...intimate level.

MARGARET. *(aside to* **MRS. GOODMAN***)* Him and me both, sister.

HEARST. Tom has proposed to me the idea of a merger of our holdings in the motion picture industry. Over the past two days, I can safely say that Tom has proven himself to be one of the most insightful and...observant people I've ever met – someone I'd be most confident to do business with. Now if only our legal ends can be ironed out. Eh, George? Eh, Dan?

GEORGE. *(chuckling along with the guests)* We'll see about that, W.R.

HEARST. *(with equal mock threat)* I certainly hope so.

MARION. Anywaaaaay...I call this meeting of the board of directors officially over.

(The guests titter.)

HEARST. Alright, alright – To Tom!

(The guests toast and drink.)

DIDI. Speech, Birthday Boy!

*(***INCE*** *is about to rise, one hand on his glass, the other holding a spot under his left rib cage.* **DR. GOODMAN***, sitting next to him, notices.)*

DR. GOODMAN. Are you all right, Tom?

INCE. Damn ulcer, it'll pass. *(to all:)* First of all, I'd like to thank my wonderful host and hostess for showing me some of the finest Hearstian hospitality I've ever known. *(A few "Here, here's" are heard.)* And second, I'd like to turn the tables a little bit and congratulate our W.R. He's a man who has everything money can buy –

MARION. And a few things money can't buy.

(The guests laugh.)

INCE. *(a nod to Marion:)* Well put. However, this weekend, I've come to realize it simply doesn't matter. W.R. came into our closed community not with stomping feet set on conquest, but with open arms and an equally open mind set on learning all about this wonderful land of make-believe. Without a superior bone in his body, he is one of us. *(raising his glass)* Speaking for the children in this exclusive playground, we're glad to have you in our lives, an equal among us. *(a beat)* To W.R.

(The guests toast **HEARST** *and drink.)*

MARION. Enough of the mutual admiration society. The *real* thing on everyone's mind is whether or not Willie will let us have a second glass of champagne.

(The guests chuckle, all eyes turning to **HEARST**. *His smile slowly drops as he surveys the expectant faces, staring at him.)*

HEARST. *(his eyes now on* **MARION***)* Is that really what's on everyone's mind?…A second glass of champagne?…

*(***MARION*** *says nothing, caught in his gaze.)*

DIDI. It's on *my* mind, I can tell you that much.

(The guests titter, but grow silent as **HEARST** *fails to respond, his eyes on* **MARION**. *When* **HEARST** *speaks, we wonder: Is he speaking to his guests...or just to* **MARION**?)

HEARST. I do not ask much. But the little I do ask...must be respected. I don't mean this as a threat. This is simply a wish I have as a man. *(becoming nervous as he surveys the bewildered faces of his guests)* I am a man asking you to behave according to my wishes...on my boat. Is that so difficult?

*(***HEARST*** looks at his silent guests for another moment, a disconnected look on his face. He panics at he painful awkwardness he has created. Suddenly, he remembers* **MARION***'s call for "The Charleston" the previous evening. He aggressively slams both fists on the table and sings:)*

HEARST. Charleston! Charleston! Da da-da da da dum...

(He continues booming out "The Charleston" until the offstage jazz band joins in full swing. One by one, the guests rise and dance, **HEARST***'s singing and table-pounding constant throughout. He does not let up until the very last guest is up and dancing.)*

(The guests dance with great energy and relieved merriment. **CELIA** *snatches the bowler from* **CHAPLIN***'s head and mimics his patented "Little Tramp walk" to the rhythms of the music.* **DIDI** *joins in followed by* **MARION** *who cannot seem to get the waddle and hip-shimmy down successfully.)*

*(***CHAPLIN*** takes great delight in this. He comes up behind* **MARION** *to guide her body into a successful "tramp walk." He places his hands on* **MARION***'s hips, directing her through the motions. She stumbles,* **CHAPLIN** *helps her. They continue their impromptu comic dance routine the guests take pleasure. For the first time, the innocent tramp's shuffle has become an accidental tool of flirtation.)*

(*INCE glances over at* **HEARST**. *The old man is boil-ing beneath the surface, staring at* **CHAPLIN** *and* **MARION**.)

CHAPLIN. (*crowning* **MARION** *with the bowler*) Ladies and Gen-tleman! I give you Marion Davies – The New Tramp.

(*They both take several bows as the guests applaud and cheer. The music and jubilation hits its highest peak. The guests filter out in various directions.*)

(*All lights fade except for one behind* **HEARST**, *leaving him an ominous silhouette. He wanders out last.*)

(*After a few moments,* **LOLLY** *re-enters and crosses to her ping-pong paddles, where she had left them. She hears voices off.*)

MARION. (*O.S.*) Let's go in here, Charlie. We can be alone.

(*Intrigued,* **LOLLY** *scoots under the long table, in hiding from* **MARION**, *who enters followed by* **CHAPLIN**, *still wearing his party hat.*)

CHAPLIN. Now why would you want to do a thing like that?

MARION. (*no reply*) Are you going ashore in the morning?

CHAPLIN. (*moving towards her*) First thing. The picture's behind schedule. I can use all the daylight I can get.

(*He removes the bowler cap, places it down, and puts his arms on* **MARION**'s *shoulders.*)

MARION. Please don't. I need…time.

CHAPLIN. Time to reconsider?

MARION. No…it's just that…a lot's happened in very little time. I know you don't want to hear this but I loved Willie – or still love him. You know what my mother always said? Romantic love fades. Marry for friendship and security.

CHAPLIN. Except you're not married. Willie is.

MARION. Christ, Charlie, my head's all over the place. Would you respect me if I didn't take time to think things through? (*She looks into* **CHAPLIN**'s *skeptical eyes.*) Hey, have a little faith in me…please?

CHAPLIN. You know, Marion, I wrote you the love letter of the century in my cabin last night. Loud and passionate, it was filled with trumpets. Victory over God through the conquest of your love!

MARION. Sounds like a helluva letter.

CHAPLIN. I became bored very quickly. It's filled with embarrassing clichés, adolescent rhyme schemes, and a repellent lack of imagination. I'm grateful to you for allowing me time to give it a second draft.

MARION. *(after a short smile:)* What about the baby, Charlie?

CHAPLIN. I intend to provide for the child.

MARION. That's not quite the same thing as being the kid's father.

CHAPLIN. I'll do what I can.

MARION. And so will Willie. He's liable to turn this Lita thing into the biggest scandal ever just to get even.

CHAPLIN. Quite a few in the press know already. If there hasn't been a scandal yet, I don't see what –

MARION. *(interrupting)* Oh no, that's where I'm the expert. You don't hang around Willie as long as I have without a little of his putrid newspaper business rubbing off on you. You see, you getting Lita pregnant is no scandal – I mean, it's illegal, technically – but no scandal as far as the papers and readers are concerned. What *is* a scandal is if you don't marry her. Worse still: if you desert her and run off with some blonde starlet. That's what they're waiting to rip you to pieces about.

CHAPLIN. How your eyes light up foretelling my doom. *(a beat)* I thought Lita's unformed quality was what I needed. There's a creative fire that ignites when you can feel yourself actually molding someone's life. Do you know that I shot literally miles of footage of her in this picture that may be completely unusable?

MARION. That's not her fault, is it?

CHAPLIN. I've stated my intentions to correct *my* mistake. I will fight these money hungry creatures who want me to marry her until the very end.

MARION. And what happens if at "the very end"...you lose?

CHAPLIN. *(a thoughtful pause)* Then, when you see me, please look the other way, because you will be looking at a man who no longer exits. Have I made myself perfectly clear?

MARION. Yes.

CHAPLIN. Good. *(after a moment or two)* Listen to us. We're both so afraid of these...persecuting forces. We've just got to say to hell with them, and pointing fingers, and bad press, and rise above it all because we believe in *us*. That's what's important. That's what matters.

MARION. *(confused)* Charlie...

CHAPLIN. I know, I know. I'm sorry. Time. Yes, I remember. Time.

(They stare into each other's eyes a moment longer.)

CHAPLIN. I'll go now.

(He kisses her slowly, gently, on the lips and starts for the exit.)

CHAPLIN. Just be careful, Marion. Time not only helps one think...but it helps one forget.

MARION. Don't worry. I'm not the forgetful type.

*(**CHAPLIN** exits.)*

*(Now "alone" in the room, **MARION** sits on the downstage edge of the table, facing the audience. After a moment, **INCE** enters.)*

INCE. Marion?

MARION. *(She whirls, startled, then relieved.)* Oh. Tom. It's you.

INCE. Who were you expecting?

MARION. No one. I had a chill for a moment.

*(**INCE** crosses to the upstage side of the table, behind **MARION**, speaking to the back of her head which still faces us.)*

INCE. Marion, I have to speak frankly with you. If I'm going to be overseeing production of your pictures, I need for us to come to terms about a few things. Things that are worrying W.R..

MARION. Like…?

*(**INCE** has spotted Chaplin's bowler cap. He places it on his own head and sits down beside her.)*

INCE. You and Charlie.

*(**MARION** does not respond.)*

INCE. Marion. I know this isn't easy, and I don't mean to pry.

MARION. Don't you?

INCE. *(sincerely)* No. And I'll be the first to admit that I've had my own share of indiscretions. But I have to know the truth from you in order to balance your needs with those of our friend, Willie. *(A beat as **MARION** maintains her silence.)* He will find out, Marion. And when he does, I'd rather be an ally who can help you.

MARION. Charlie had…certain feelings for me, but…I've convinced him that it's useless for him to pursue me.

INCE. Certain feelings? Has he told you he loves you?

*(At this moment, with **MARION** and **INCE** next to each other and facing downstage, **HEARST** appears behind them, facing their backs. **MARION** proceeds, overly glib in order to convince **INCE**.)*

MARION. He says he loves me, but there was never any love, at least not from my side there wasn't. I don't love him and I never have.

*(**HEARST**'s eyes are glazed over. Given Ince's size, Chaplin's bowler, and the intimacy of their bodies, **HEARST** believes that **MARION** is admitting her lack of feelings for him to her lover – Chaplin. At a complete loss, he raises the diamond-studded revolver.)*

HEARST. Chaplin!

(Before either **MARION** *or* **INCE** *can turn their heads – * **HEARST** *fires the gun.* **LOLLY** *screams. Clutching his head,* **INCE** *turns around to face* **HEARST** *before collapsing.)*

HEARST. My God...

(Blackout)

Scene 4

(Main Dining Room. **INCE** *is lying on his back on the long table. Immobile. Aided by* **WILLICOMBE**, **DR. GOODMAN** *is bandaging* **INCE**'s *bloody head, a medical supply kit beside him.)*

*(***HEARST** *and* **MARION** *are in the room, both devastated, at separate sides of the room.* **HEARST** *now holds the gun impotently in his hand.* **LOLLY** *is gone.)*

(After several moments of silence, **DR. GOODMAN** *finishes his bandaging and steps back, looking up at* **HEARST**.*)*

DR. GOODMAN. There's nothing more I can do for him, W.R. We must get him ashore or there's no hope for him at all.

WILLICOMBE. W.R.?

*(***HEARST** *looks up, saying nothing.)*

*(***MARION** *rises and crosses to* **HEARST**, *lifting him to his feet. For the first time since we've seen him, he seems like both an old man and a frightened child.)*

MARION. Come on, Pops, let's stand up.

(She guides him to downstage left to speak to him in confidence.)

MARION. Willie?

HEARST. It's Tom…

MARION. Willie.

HEARST. That's Tom…on my table…

MARION. Willie. Hey, Willie, look at me. *(He does.)* You've got to be strong here.

HEARST. What…why…did you say…there was never any love?

MARION. It wasn't about you.

HEARST. Who then?

MARION. *(a beat)* Charlie. Tom noticed that Charlie's been sniffing around. I told him I didn't love *Charlie*.

HEARST. Is that true?

MARION. Yes, that's who I was talking about.

(He stares at her, reading her eyes. After a moment, he leans in hugging her for dear life.)

MARION. We'll make it. You can handle this. Whatever happens…I'll be by your side.

HEARST. Do you see? You are my whole world.

MARION. Oh, Willie…

(They remain in the embrace as our attention shifts back to **WILLICOMBE** *and* **DR. GOODMAN**.*)*

WILLICOMBE. Is he going to die?

DR. GOODMAN. Maybe.

WILLICOMBE. God help us.

DR. GOODMAN. God's who we work for.

WILLICOMBE. Since the Fatty Arbuckle mess, The Hays Office is cracking down on *everything*, no matter who's involved.

DR. GOODMAN. Don't be ridiculous. The Hays Office is run by the Republican Party chairman.

WILLICOMBE. I know who Will Hays is.

DR. GOODMAN. If it wasn't for the support of Hearst newspapers, do you think Coolidge would've been elected President two weeks ago? Or Harding before him? No my friend, Will Hays does not want to put William Randolph Hearst in jail. If anything, he'll help him stay out. After all, it's just Tom Ince, right? Who's Tom Ince next to two Presidents and the most powerful newspaper man in the world?

WILLICOMBE. Just a man.

DR. GOODMAN. Less than that, I'm afraid.

*(**HEARST**/**MARION***'s embrace ends.)*

HEARST. What are his chances, Dan?

DR. GOODMAN. It's difficult to say. There doesn't seem to be an exit wound.

HEARST. You mean the bullet's still in his head?

DR. GOODMAN. I believe so.

HEARST. The bastard's tough as a bull.

DR. GOODMAN. A bullet in the head is a funny thing.

HEARST. I don't hear Tom laughing.

DR. GOODMAN. What I mean is, Lincoln, for example, didn't actually die for some time after being shot. If they knew more about brains and bullets, he just might have survived.

HEARST. Abraham Lincoln's been dead sixty years and Tom Ince is still alive. I want it to stay that way. *(He stands over* **INCE** *for a moment.)* Lincoln was overrated.

*(***HEARST** *abruptly exits.)*

(Blackout.)

Scene 5

(Main Dining Room set. **INCE**'s *body is gone, the blood cleaned up. Only* **HEARST, MARION** *and* **WILLICOMBE** *are present. The ship-to-shore radio is set up on the table where Ince's body once was.* **MRS. INCE** *is not seen. Her voice something crackling that floats in the air over the ship-to-shore.)*

MRS. INCE'S VOICE. Hello?

HEARST. Nel? W.R. Hearst here.

MRS. INCE'S VOICE. Mr. Hearst, how are you?

HEARST. I'm fine, Nel. Unfortunately, there's a problem with Tom, darling – are you sitting?

MRS. INCE'S VOICE. Yes, I am, oh dear God.

HEARST. Tom's had an accident, love, a bad one.

MRS. INCE'S VOICE. What sort of accident?

HEARST. Nel, I don't know how to tell you this except to start by saying Tom's been very depressed about his business lately and...I hate to be the one to tell you, Nel...he's been unfaithful to you.

MRS. INCE'S VOICE. *(beginning to sob)* Oh, Lord...what's happened?

HEARST. Now, Nel, you've got to be brave. He's taken to her very strongly and, to the best of my knowledge... she tried to end it.

MRS. INCE'S VOICE. Please...please...

HEARST. Nel, he...God-save-'im, he shot himself.

MRS. INCE'S VOICE. Tom?! My Tom?!

HEARST. Now, Nel, he's alive and getting the best of care. Our Dr. Goodman is escorting him to your home by private ambulance. *(silence)* Nel?

MRS. INCE'S VOICE. *(going into shock)* I...I'm here.

HEARST. Nel, I want you to give me the name of his private physician – can you do that?

MRS. INCE'S VOICE. *(still dazed)* Yes...Dr. Ida Glasgow...oh, Tom...

HEARST. Nel, by God, we're going to do our damnedest to keep what happened out of the papers, for dear Tom's sake and for the sake of your lovely family.

MRS. INCE'S VOICE. *(panicking)* Oh my God, we have to! We have to!

HEARST. Now, calm down, Nel, and stay where you are. We will make sure no one finds out. You've got to remain strong and silent and wait for Dr. Glasgow to give you instructions. We'll call him and have him by your side in no time at all.

MRS. INCE'S VOICE. Bless you, Mr. Hearst...I'll wait for the doctor...bless you...Oh. Tom...

HEARST. No one will ever find out. You have my word on that, Nel. Tom's friendship means too much to me.

MRS. INCE'S VOICE. I'm sorry? His what?

HEARST. *(louder)* His friendship! *(softer)* We're telling them it's his stomach, his ulcers.

MRS. INCE'S VOICE. Yes, his ulcers...oh, Tom...

HEARST. I'm going to hang up now, Nel, and call Dr. Glasgow. He and I will take care of everything. You just sit and wait.

MRS. INCE'S VOICE. Yes...his ulcers...I'll just sit and wait... oh, Tom...

HEARST. Goodbye, Nel.

MRS. INCE'S VOICE. Oh, Tom...

HEARST. Goodbye.

(**HEARST** *nods to* **WILLICOMBE** *who disconnects* **MRS. INCE**.)

MRS. INCE'S VOICE. Oh my poor –

WILLICOMBE. Shall I call Dr. Glasgow now?

HEARST. *(checking his watch)* We have to move all this back to the bridge. The guests will be coming in for breakfast soon.

(**WILLICOMBE** *begins to pack up the ship-to-shore equipment.* **HEARST** *approaches a physically and emotionally drained* **MARION**.)

HEARST. Marion, in a short time, we'll have to address our guests.

MARION. Oh no, Willie, please. I can't…I just can't…

HEARST. You said you'd be at my side through this. You certainly have to be now. Otherwise, they'll suspect something happened.

MARION. Something *did* happen and I'm not strong enough to tell them just yet.

HEARST. *(takes a moment to gather his thoughts)* There is something you have to understand, Marion. Tom Ince suffered an ulcerous attack this morning so I asked Dr. Goodman to escort him home by train.

MARION. What…what are you…

HEARST. Just say it: Tom Ince suffered an ulcerous –

MARION. *(interrupting)* You can't hide this, Willie. Fairy tales to soothe Nel Ince are one thing, but for God's sake, you put a bullet into a movie studio head! You think no one's gonna notice?!

HEARST. *(trying to contain his anger)* There is no movie studio head with a bullet in him.

MARION. Well I say differently!

HEARST. *(exploding) No you don't!* You don't say differently, do differently, or act differently than I tell you to – not now and not ever!

MARION. *(not recognizing this man)* What is this? What are you saying to me?

HEARST. I am telling you what must be. Here and now. *My* needs. *Final.*

MARION. It's just pretend, isn't it? Coming down from up there…playing with us humans for a little while… Something like this happens and there you go…back up in the sky. I had such hopes for you, Pops.

HEARST. I love you, Marion, but if you fail to stand by me through this, I'll…I'll…

MARION. You'll what? Say it.

HEARST. I will pull the rug out from under your life in ways you never dreamed possible. Your career. Your family. Your world. *Everything.*

MARION. Such hopes, Pops...such high hopes.

HEARST. Tom Ince suffered an ulcerous attack. That is
not a story that I will have to "make" anyone believe,
because that is what, in fact, happened. And I will
break any man, woman, or child who says differently.

MARION. You'd break me, too, Willie?

HEARST. *(a beat)* I am William Randolph Hearst and I do
not drown for anyone.

(**HEARST**, **MARION**, *and* **WILLICOMBE** *remain where
they stand. Lights slowly fade to darkness.*)

Scene 6

(A Cabin. Only **HEARST** *and* **LOLLY** *are present.)*

HEARST. You're looking...well rested.

LOLLY. Yes, I must say, whatever Dr. Goodman gave me put me right to sleep, thank goodness.

HEARST. So, you're feeling better now.

LOLLY. Much.

HEARST. I'm so glad.

(A moment of silence as they each maintain a fixed, unblinking gaze.)

LOLLY. It was a tragic accident, Mr. Hearst.

HEARST. Yes, Lolly.

LOLLY. *(a beat)* But, these things doooo happen, as they say.

HEARST. That they do.

LOLLY. It's no one's fault, really, when you consider all sides.

HEARST. You're very good at that – considering all sides.

LOLLY. You meet so few people in life who are capable of considering all sides.

HEARST. One could almost call it a gift.

LOLLY. One could. *(a beat)* You know, I must confess, and I know I've been a bit obvious – do you have a second to talk?

HEARST. I have two and one half minutes.

LOLLY. Well, I was going to break one of your first rules and mix business with pleasure this weekend by asking you about expanding my syndication with a more prominent by-line. I really felt that's what I needed to better serve this wonderful motion –

HEARST. *(interrupting)* Well, Lolly, why didn't you just say so, of course we can arrange –

LOLLY. (**LOLLY** *is now the first guest to dare cut-off* **HEARST**.) Well, I didn't say anything because I started thinking – the only way I can *really* have an effect is to gain the trust of the readers *and* the community I'm covering. And that takes time. Lots of time.

HEARST. I agree with you one hundred percent. I'll have my office draw up an eight-year contract at –

LOLLY. W.R., now really. Eight years won't do either of us any good. We both are at a point in our careers where we have a need for security.

HEARST. Security? From whom?

LOLLY. The wrong people. There are wrong people you know.

HEARST. Yes. I know.

LOLLY. I'm willing to devote my life to Hearst newspapers. I have to know here and now if you'll grant me the life I want. You give me my security...and I'll give you yours...for a lifetime.

HEARST. You're suggesting...a lifetime contract?

LOLLY. Well. *(a beat)* I wouldn't call it a suggestion, W.R.

(**HEARST** *looks at her. An admiring smile forming.*)

(Blackout.)

Scene 7

(Same Main Dining Room set except breakfast is laid out. **ELINOR, MARGARET, GEORGE THOMAS, DIDI, CELIA,** *and* **CHAPLIN** *filter into the room.)*

CELIA. Some people will say anything to get attention.

DIDI. I swear I heard a shot.

ELINOR. Oh Didi!

DIDI. I did!

ELINOR. Was it close to your cabin?

CELIA. Trust me, folks, the only shot Didi was close to had whisky in it.

DIDI. Oh, be quiet. I know what I heard.

ELINOR. Well who are we missing, exactly?

GEORGE. Mr. Hearst, for one. Miss Davies.

DIDI. Big Joe Willicombe.

MARGARET. I haven't seen Tom.

CELIA. The doc and his old lady.

ELINOR. And Louella Parsons.

CHAPLIN. *(correcting her)* Lolly.

GEORGE. Where could they all be?

DIDI. Well, I don't know what's going on, but I'm telling you – I heard a gunshot or a bang or something.

ELINOR. I suspect we should all continue eating and when we have devoured the very last morsel, W.R. and the others will pop into the room with a sufficiently exciting story with which to beguile us.

(Behind the guests, **HEARST** *appears.* **MARION** *and* **WIL-LICOMBE** *are at his side.)*

*(***MARION** *remains stone-faced throughout, making little or no effort to support* **HEARST**. *She avoids eye contact with* **CHAPLIN** *despite his efforts.)*

HEARST. Credit us with better manners than that, Elinor.

ELINOR. There you all are.

MARGARET. Where's Tom?

CELIA. On a row boat with Lolly Parsons, it would seem.

*(**DIDI** and **CELIA** titter.)*

HEARST. No, I'm afraid there's no "sufficiently exciting story with which to beguile you." Tom Ince took ill late last night and had to be taken off the boat.

GEORGE. What?

MARGARET. What was wrong with him?

HEARST. Stomach pains.

GEORGE. Why didn't someone call me?

HEARST. We wanted to. Believe me. But Tom asked us not to trouble you in the middle of the night. Not to worry – Dr. Goodman is accompanying him home to his wife and children as we speak.

ELINOR. Oh that's terrible, just terrible. And Miss Parsons?

*(**HEARST** is stumped for a moment. **MARION** offers no support.)*

HEARST. Lolly...helped Tom through his difficulties – Lolly's got ulcers herself – so she was up very late and is still resting.

DIDI. Well, we all must go up and visit Tom this week, the poor birthday boy.

HEARST. That's a splendid idea. There is one thing that I must ask you all and I can't say it with enough serious-ness. To our eyes, Tom Ince left this boat with a bout of angry ulcers. However, I can't begin to imagine what the press will make up. A wild birthday party, excessive alcohol, orgies...

*(**DIDI** and **CELIA** giggle once again.)*

Oh you might laugh now, but let's not forget the scan-dal of our Fatty Arbuckle. Acquitted – yes...but a career ruined. I just feel it would be best for all of us if no one says anything about what happened on board this weekend. As a newspaper man, I can tell you, they're out for your blood. They'll link Tom's innocent ulcers to every little secret every one of us in this room has ever kept and drag us all down.

(A moment as he looks over the genuinely concerned faces of his guests.)

HEARST. So I'm asking all of you to take an oath of silence with me – you were sleeping, you left early, whatever excuse you want – but you do not know what happened to Tom Ince on board this boat.

(A dead silence falls over the room. After a few moments:)

ELINOR. This is most dramatic, W.R.! Deliciously theatrical!

CELIA. I for one would love to take the oath – I have reporters *still* hounding me about what *really* happened during the orgy scene in "Intolerance."

DIDI. Me, too! Me, too! I'll take the oath of silence!

HEARST. Thank you, ladies. And now before we depart from what was, for the most part, a splendid weekend, do I have all of your oaths of silence?

(The guests chime in their compliance. All except CHAP-LIN. No one but HEARST and MARION notice this.)

HEARST. Very well. I'm sure I speak for Tom when I say thank you all for coming and making Tom's birthday such a memorable time. Cars will be at the dock shortly; why don't we all pack up and meet on deck in an hour.

(Again, ad libs of agreement as the guests file out of the room. As the rest leave ahead of her, MARGARET pauses in the doorway, turning to HEARST.)

MARGARET. Excuse me, Mr. Hearst, but you are sure Tom is all right, aren't you?

HEARST. He'll be just fine, Miss Livingston. You know, I meant to tell you all weekend – you really are quite a fine actress.

MARGARET. Thank you, but if Tom wasn't feeling well, he would have –

HEARST. Please don't worry about Tom. He's getting the best of care. We really should meet at the studio. God, you're good. I saw you in that picture. You played the lovely young woman. What was it called? Oh, I don't remember the title, but you were splendid. Can you come by next week? *(checking with* **WILLICOMBE***)* Friday? *(***WILLICOMBE** *nods.)* Friday. How about it?

MARGARET. *(dazed)* Friday?...uhm...

*(***HEARST** *puts his arm around* **MARGARET** *and leads her away for a private moment.)*

HEARST. I want you to know that Tom spoke very...lovingly about you and wanted you to know how sorry he was that this happened.

MARGARET. But why wasn't I awakened? Why didn't he want me to accompany him?

HEARST. Accompany him? Child, you're his mistress. You can't accompany Tom home to greet his wife and children. *(***MARGARET** *is speechless.)* Don't worry. Tom is fine and your secret is safe. That's what's important. *(ushering her to the door)* See you Friday.

(Still in a daze, **MARGARET** *exits.)*

(As **HEARST** *turns to face the room, he finds that along with* **MARION** *and* **WILLICOMBE***, only* **CHAPLIN** *remains, his feet boldly crossed on top of the table.* **MARION** *is also in the room, still silent since her entrance.)*

HEARST. *(to* **WILLICOMBE***:)* You've got things to do.

*(***WILLICOMBE** *nods and leaves the room.)*

*(***HEARST** *and* **CHAPLIN** *remain staring at each other in complete silence, neither man saying a word...until:)*

HEARST. What do you think you know?

CHAPLIN. Why, W.R., whatever do you mean?

HEARST. All my guests have left the room. You're here.

CHAPLIN. Didi thinks she heard a gunshot, and I did, too.

HEARST. I can't help what you and Didi think you heard.

CHAPLIN. My man, Kono, has been parked on the dock since daybreak. He says he saw the injured man taken off the boat. An injured man who he thought was me. A man with blood on his head – hardly an ulcer.

HEARST. *(after a beat)* What do you want, Charlie?

CHAPLIN. You had no reason to shoot Tom Ince. You *did* have a reason to shoot a man who *looked* like him – Me.

HEARST. Why the hell would I want to shoot you?

CHAPLIN. You've had suspicions about me and Marion and they were confirmed for you by the article which you left for her to discover.

HEARST. Too many words, Charlie; just spit it out.

CHAPLIN. You shot Tom Ince.

(HEARST stares at him a moment and then bursts into loud laughter. He lowers himself into a chair near CHAPLIN.)

HEARST. What do you want, Charlie?

CHAPLIN. That's not an answer.

(HEARST places a wrapped stack of bills on the table between himself and CHAPLIN.)

HEARST. I have no time for rumors or to argue them. How much do you want to keep this "theory" of yours in this room?

CHAPLIN. Do you really insist on insulting me?

HEARST. Name your price and don't waste my time.

CHAPLIN. What makes you so certain it's money I want from you?

HEARST. *(He takes pause, weighing this last statement.)* There is…something else that belongs to me that you wish to possess?

CHAPLIN. *(a beat of hesitation, then:)* Let her go and you'll have my silence.

HEARST. *(amused)* "Let her go?"

(HEARST looks from CHAPLIN to MARION who is looking away, unwilling to lend her voice.)

HEARST. Are you going somewhere, Marion?

(MARION does not respond.)

HEARST. You should take that as a "No," Charlie.

CHAPLIN. Marion, say something.

*(**MARION** says nothing. There is silence for a moment or two. Then, **HEARST** breaks the stillness with a loud laugh.)*

HEARST. It's amazing how unaware some men are of what they *truly* want most.

*(**HEARST** takes out two more one-inch thick stacks of bills from his pocket and places them on the table.)*

HEARST. This is what you really want, Charlie. This is what you need. This will finish your movie, protect you if it flops like the last one, cover all the ugly expenses Lita is putting you through. This will give you peace.

CHAPLIN. Do you mistake me for a boat, a chain of newspapers, or some exotic statue? Do you think you can just keep slapping stacks of money on the table until you never shot Tom Ince at all?

HEARST. Yes.

*(**CHAPLIN** abruptly rises, intending to leave.)*

CHAPLIN. To hell with you both.

HEARST. Lita is an ugly story, Charlie.

*(This stops **CHAPLIN** dead in his tracks.)*

HEARST. A little girl, thirteen, fourteen years old -

CHAPLIN. Sixteen.

HEARST. Fine, sixteen. And I sympathize with you, really I do. I mean, if I were a bastard, I'd say that I'd keep your little scandal out of my papers in exchange for your silence. But I have more respect for you than that. I know that isn't what you really care about. What you *really* care about is your work, your artistry. Making movies, Charlie. Finishing "The Gold Rush." That is what you want most, isn't it?

*(A beat of silence as **CHAPLIN** offers no reply.)*

You see, that's what I can stop you from doing. Finishing the picture. Or ever making pictures again. One word from me and your financiers will never talk to you again. One ugly story about you published by me and your audience will never want to *see* you again. Just one word in the ear of a banker or in America's morning paper. You do believe me, don't you? Well, don't you?

CHAPLIN. Yes.

HEARST. Good, because I not only offer you sympathetic coverage in my papers but a continuing supply of hard cash during your troubled artistic and personal times. And rest assured, Charlie, my reserves come from a bottomless well that never runs dry. Besides, you didn't really see anything, did you? Your Japanese driver *thinks* he saw the color red on Ince's forehead. That's all I'm buying from you. Now you ask anyone and they'd tell you you're robbing old Hearst blind.

(**HEARST** *rises.* **CHAPLIN** *remains silent.* **MARION** *continues to look away, her eyes glazed over.*)

HEARST. I don't need an answer from you yet. You collect your things and go at your leisure. But if those little pieces of green paper are gone when you leave...I'll have my answer. Goodbye, Charlie.

(**HEARST** *heads for the door. He stops in the doorway. Without turning around:*)

HEARST. Marion?

(*For the first time,* **MARION** *turns her head and looks directly at* **CHAPLIN**. *Now it is* **CHAPLIN** *who can't return the gaze. After a moment, she turns and walks out of the room ahead of* **HEARST**, *who follows.*)

(**CHAPLIN** *is alone in the room, sitting across several wrapped bundles of money. Silence. He slowly reaches forward and grabs the first stack...then the second...*)

(**ELINOR** *appears, addressing the audience.*)

ELINOR. I don't know that Charlie took any money from Hearst. The whisper is that we all took something away that weekend. But I think most of us left more behind than we ever got in return.

(*Lights fade on* **CHAPLIN** *but remain on* **ELINOR**.)

ELINOR. *(addressing the audience)* Like others with tiny bullets hiding in their skulls, Thomas Ince held on for two days, unconscious, before dying in his own bed. There was plenty of misinformation in the days that followed, much of it coming straight from the Hearst press machine which inexplicably reported that Ince was "stricken unconscious" while visiting Hearst at his upstate ranch. Three weeks later, the San Diego District Attorney conducted an obligatory investigation and was – quote – satisfied that the death of Thomas H. Ince was caused by heart failure as a result of acute indigestion – unquote. He did not examine the body, because Tom was cremated immediately, and except for Dr. Goodman, not a single member of the boating party was ever questioned, including Hearst. The San Diego D.A. suggested that the Los Angeles office continue the investigation. They politely declined.

(As **ELINOR** *speaks of people –* **MARGARET, LOLLY, CHAPLIN, MARION, HEARST** *– they should drift in or be illuminated in some fashion.)*

ELINOR. After Tom's death, Margaret Livingston's salary mysteriously jumped from three hundred dollars to one thousand dollars a week. Lolly got her lifetime contract and, for the next twenty-five years, became the most powerful and feared columnist in America. Three days after attending Tom's funeral, Charlie married Lita Grey in Mexico. It lasted two years. He did, however, dismiss her from the cast of "The Gold Rush" and re-shoot all her scenes. Despite costing a small fortune, the picture was a smashing success. It took three more years for W.R. to let Marion do a full-fledged comedy. As Charlie predicted, she triumphed. She remained by Hearst's side for the next twenty-seven years, right up until his death. *(a beat)* To this day, no two accounts of that weekend cruise are the same, including who, in fact, was on the boat. There are no logs, you see, no records or photographs of any kind. And, as Hearst requested, not a single person involved wrote or spoke about that weekend…that is…until significantly after the old man's death, and even then only in riddles. *(a beat)* The California Curse. You see, to recognize it is not the same as avoiding its spell.

(As she continues, the remaining cast members – INCE included – drift onstage, dancing the Charleston in surreal slow motion. Only INCE does not dance, remaining aloof, watching the others.)

ELINOR. I've had a recurring dream recently: I'm in a beautiful ballroom, having a glorious time dancing The Charleston. But I'm watching how ridiculous everyone *else* looks and I wonder why they don't realize it. Then I catch my own reflection in a mirror and see that, in fact, I too look like a fool. Yet, it's so much fun…that none of us can stop. *(a beat)* If we stopped…

(The entire dancing cast freezes in tableaux.)

ELINOR. We'd have nothing.

(Lights slowly fade to black on the tableaux.)

End of Play

PROP LIST

ACT I

Scene 1 – balloons, a pin, clipboard

Scene 2 – Hearst's gun, case for gun

Scene 3 – champagne glasses

Scene 4 – Celia's small box, bottle of alcohol (unlabeled), a marijuana cigarette, three small pieces of paper for Elinor, Small slip of paper for Willicombe

ACT II

Scene 1 – a shoe, Willicombe's small slip of paper from I:4 (now in Marion's possession)

Scene 2 – two ping-pong paddles

Scene 3 – 13 party hats of differing varieties with specifics indicated in the text, champagne glasses, Hearst's gun

Scene 4 – doctor's kit, bandage stained with blood,

Scene 5 – ship to shore radio, microphone

Scene 6 – N/A

Scene 7 – coffee cups, bowl of fruit, wrapped bundles of money

From the Reviews of
THE CAT'S MEOW...

"HEARST YACHT MYSTERY IS THE 'CAT'S MEOW'! A stylish and sardonically funny expose of corrupt Tinseltown values... Sophisticated decadence and full steam momentum."
- *Los Angeles Times*

"STEVEN PEROS' INTRIGUING FICTIONALIZED SPECULATION imagines the worst as everyone cavorts through an oceanic orgy of intrigue, seduction, infidelity, blackmail, booze, drugs, and murder!...What titillating action it is!"
- *Daily Variety*

"RECOMMENDED - HANDS DOWN! Will have you on the edge of your seat...Peros certainly knows how to write believable dialogue... A very fine ensemble piece."
- Tom Hatten, CBS Radio

"A TERRIFIC NEW DRAMA!" - Marilyn Beck, *Daily News*

"STEVEN PEROS' NEW PLAY ABOUT THE CATTY SIDE OF HOLLYWOOD TRULY IS *THE CAT'S MEOW*! This tart little snippet of history mystery is full of wicked humor and tawdry tales... Peros' dialog and retorts are what makes this play work so well. Nearly everyone is up to something and all are trying to hide it."
- *Santa Monica Outlook*

PURRS WITH OLD TIME GLITZ AND LARGER THAN LIFE CHARACTERS...A stylish and intriguing play, toying with conspiracy theories but leaving its mark in its wry portrayals of history's glitziest figures ... Peros weaves his theories together with a humor and fast-paced wit that befits the roaring 20s...Puts the dark glamour that made 'L.A. Confidential' so intriguing, on stage."
- *Daily Bruin*

"A STYLISH DARK COMEDY...This cleverly conceived fictionalization presents one intriguing theory to a legendary unsolved mystery...Peros' script is engrossing and amusing...A pleasant escapist diversion for those who revel in nostalgia and tabloid-style scandal."
- *4FRONT MAGAZINE*

OTHER TITLES AVAILABLE FROM SAMUEL FRENCH

MAURITIUS
Theresa Rebeck

Comedy / 3m, 2f / Interior
Stamp collecting is far more risky than you think. After their mother's death, two estranged half-sisters discover a book of rare stamps that may include the crown jewel for collectors. One sister tries to collect on the windfall, while the other resists for sentimental reasons. In this gripping tale, a seemingly simple sale becomes dangerous when three seedy, high-stakes collectors enter the sisters' world, willing to do anything to claim the rare find as their own.

"(Theresa Rebeck's) belated Broadway bow, the only original play by a woman to have its debut on Broadway this fall."
- Robert Simonson, *New York Times*

"*Mauritius* caters efficiently to a hunger that Broadway hasn't been gratifying in recent years. That's the corkscrew-twist drama of suspense… she has strewn her script with a multitude of mysteries."
- Ben Brantley, *New York Times*

"Theresa Rebeck is a slick playwright… Her scenes have a crisp shape, her dialogue pops, her characters swagger through an array of showy emotion, and she knows how to give a plot a cunning twist."
- John Lahr, *The New Yorker*

OTHER TITLES AVAILABLE FROM SAMUEL FRENCH

ADRIFT IN MACAO
Book and Lyrics by Christopher Durang
Music by Peter Melnick

Full Length / Musical / 4m, 3f / Unit Sets

Set in 1952 in Macao, China, *Adrift In Macao* is a loving parody of film noir movies. Everyone that comes to Macao is waiting for something, and though none of them know exactly what that is, they hang around to find out. The characters include your film noir standards, like Laureena, the curvacious blonde, who luckily bumps into Rick Shaw, the cynical surf and turf casino owner her first night in town. She ends up getting a job singing in his night club – perhaps for no reason other than the fact that she looks great in a slinky dress. And don't forget about Mitch, the American who has just been framed for murder by the mysterious villain McGuffin. With songs and quips, puns and farcical shenanigans, this musical parody is bound to please audiences of all ages.

OTHER TITLES AVAILABLE FROM SAMUEL FRENCH

GUTENBERG! THE MUSICAL!
Scott Brown and Anthony King

2m / Musical Comedy

In this two-man musical spoof, a pair of aspiring playwrights perform a backers' audition for their new project - a big, splashy musical about printing press inventor Johann Gutenberg. With an unending supply of enthusiasm, Bud and Doug sing all the songs and play all the parts in their crass historical epic, with the hope that one of the producers in attendance will give them a Broadway contract – fulfilling their ill-advised dreams.

"A smashing success!"
- *The New York Times*

"Brilliantly realized and side-splitting!
- *New York Magazine*

"There are lots of genuine laughs in Gutenberg!"
- *New York Post*

SAMUEL FRENCH STAFF

Nate Collins
President

Ken Dingledine
Director of Operations,
Vice President

Bruce Lazarus
Executive Director,
General Counsel

Rita Maté
Director of Finance

ACCOUNTING
Lori Thimsen | Director of Licensing Compliance
Nehal Kumar | Senior Accounting Associate
Charles Graytok | Accounting and Finance Manager
Glenn Halcomb | Royalty Administration
Jessica Zheng | Accounts Receivable
Andy Lian | Accounts Payable
Charlie Sou | Accounting Associate
Joann Mannello | Orders Administrator

BUSINESS AFFAIRS
Caitlin Bartow | Assistant to the Executive Director

CORPORATE COMMUNICATIONS
Abbie Van Nostrand | Director of Corporate
Communications

CUSTOMER SERVICE AND LICENSING
Laura Lindson | Licensing Services Manager
Kim Rogers | Theatrical Specialist
Matthew Akers | Theatrical Specialist
Ashley Byrne | Theatrical Specialist
Jennifer Carter | Theatrical Specialist
Annette Storckman | Theatrical Specialist
Julia Izumi | Theatrical Specialist
Sarah Weber | Theatrical Specialist
Nicholas Dawson | Theatrical Specialist
David Kimple | Theatrical Specialist
Ryan McLeod | Theatrical Specialist
Carly Erickson | Theatrical Specialist

EDITORIAL
Amy Rose Marsh | Literary Manager
Ben Coleman | Literary Associate

MARKETING
Ryan Pointer | Marketing Manager
Courtney Kochuba | Marketing Associate
Chris Kam | Marketing Associate

PUBLICATIONS AND PRODUCT DEVELOPMENT
David Geer | Publications Manager
Tyler Mullen | Publications Associate
Emily Sorensen | Publications Associate
Derek P. Hassler | Musical Products Coordinator
Zachary Orts | Musical Materials Coordinator

OPERATIONS
Casey McLain | Operations Supervisor
Elizabeth Minski | Office Coordinator, Reception
Coryn Carson | Office Coordinator, Reception

SAMUEL FRENCH BOOKSHOP (LOS ANGELES)
Joyce Mehess | Bookstore Manager
Cory DeLair | Bookstore Buyer
Kristen Springer | Customer Service Manager
Tim Coultas | Bookstore Associate
Bryan Jansyn | Bookstore Associate
Alfred Contreras | Shipping & Receiving

LONDON OFFICE
Anne-Marie Ashman | Accounts Assistant
Felicity Barks | Rights & Contracts Associate
Steve Blacker | Bookshop Associate
David Bray | Customer Services Associate
Robert Cooke | Assistant Buyer
Stephanie Dawson | Amateur Licensing Associate
Simon Ellison | Retail Sales Manager
Robert Hamilton | Amateur Licensing Associate
Peter Langdon | Marketing Manager
Louise Mappley | Amateur Licensing Associate
James Nicolau | Despatch Associate
Emma Anacootee-Parmar | Production/Editorial
Controller
Martin Phillips | Librarian
Panos Panayi | Company Accountant
Zubayed Rahman | Despatch Associate
Steve Sanderson | Royalty Administration Supervisor
Douglas Schatz | Acting Executive Director
Roger Sheppard | I.T. Manager
Debbie Simmons | Licensing Sales Team Leader
Peter Smith | Amateur Licensing Associate
Garry Spratley | Customer Service Manager
David Webster | UK Operations Director
Sarah Wolf | Rights Director